THE

HEART

IN

WINTER

THE
HEART
IN
WINTER

A NOVEL

Kevin Barry

DOUBLEDAY   NEW YORK

Copyright © 2024 by Kevin Barry

All rights reserved. Published in the United States by Doubleday, a division
of Penguin Random House LLC, New York, and distributed in Canada by
Penguin Random House Canada Limited, Toronto. Originally published in
hardcover in Great Britain by Canongate Books Ltd., London, in 2024.

www.doubleday.com

DOUBLEDAY and the portrayal of an anchor with a dolphin are
registered trademarks of Penguin Random House LLC.

Library of Congress Cataloging-in-Publication Data
Names: Barry, Kevin, 1969– author.
Title: The heart in winter : a novel / Kevin Barry.
Description: First edition. | New York : Doubleday, 2024.
Identifiers: LCCN 2023030844 | ISBN 9780385550598 (hardcover) |
ISBN 9780385550604 (ebook)
Subjects: LCSH: Irish—Montana—Fiction. | LCGFT: Romance fiction. | Novels.
Classification: LCC PR6102.A7833 H43 2024 | DDC 823/.92—dc23/eng/2020728
LC record available at https://lccn.loc.gov/2023030844

Book design by Anna B. Knighton
Jacket design by Oliver Munday

MANUFACTURED IN THE UNITED STATES OF AMERICA

1 3 5 7 9 10 8 6 4 2

First American Edition

FOR OLIVIA

I do not see any beauty in self-restraint.

— MARY MACLANE

BUTTE,
MONTANA

1891

The First Encounter

On Wyoming Street in the evening a patent Irish stumbled by, some crazy old meathead in a motley of rags and filthy buckskin, wild tufts of hair sticking out the ears, the eyes burning now like hot stars, now clamped shut in a kind of ecstasy, and he lurched and tottered on broken boots like a nightmare overgrown child, like some massive obliterated eejit child, and he sang out his wares in a sweet clear lilting—

> *Pot-ay-toes?*
> *Hot po-tay-toes?*
> *Hot pot-ah-toes a pe-nny?*

His verse swung across the raw naked street and back again, and was musical, but he had no potatoes at all. Tom Rourke turned and looked after the man with great feeling. To be old and mad and forgotten on the mountain—was it all laid out the fuck ahead of him?

It was the October again. Rourke himself approached the street at this hour in suave array and manic tatters. He was nine years climbing the slow hill of Wyoming Street and there was not a single medal pinned to his chest for it. In the evening sun the East Ridge glowed sombre and gold and an ignorant wind brought news of the winter. He was appalled at the charismatic light. He marched into the cold wind. He gave out yards to himself. He rejected once more the possibility of God. His body was tense and his mind abroad. He was turned first one way, now the other. He walked as calamity. He walked under Libra. He was living all this bullshit from the inside out. Oh, he scathed himself and harangued and to his own feet flung down fresh charges. But there were dreams of escape, too—one day you could ride south on a fine horse for the Monida Pass.

In truth he was often a bit shaky at the hour of dusk and switchable of mood but there was more to it this evening. Somehow his dreams were taking on contour and heft, and the odd stirrings that he felt were deep and premonitory, as at the approach of a dangerous fate.

Now a train eerily whistled as it entered the yards of the Union Pacific and he was twitching like a motherfucker out of control.

———

By Park and Main the darkness had fallen. He looked in at the Board of Trade for a consultation. He took a glass of whiskey and a beer chaser. He slapped the one and sipped the other. The bad nerves fell away on a quick grade to calmness and resolve. He gathered himself beautifully. He took out a pad and a length of pencil. He looked to the long mirror above the bar and spoke without turning to Patrick Holohan, of Eyeries, County Cork, a miner of the Whistler pit—

Object matrimony, he said.

Holohan in turn considered the mirror warily—

Go again, Tom?

It's what we say early on. It's cards on the fucken table time. Show that you're not playing games with the girl. What's it her name is anyhow?

Holohan with native shyness slid a letter along the bartop. The wet papery flutters of his breath meant a lunger in the long run. Tom Rourke unfolded the letter and briefly read—you'd need a heart of stone in this line—and he began fluently at once to write.

This'll only be a rough go at it, he said. See if we can strike some manner of tone. Reassure the girl.

Moments passed by in the calm of composition. Looking up, briefly, in search of a word, he saw Pat Holohan in the mirror observing the work with guilt. There was terror in the man's eyes that he might have a measure of happiness due.

Dear Miss Stapleton—Rourke spoke it now as he read over the words—or Margaret, if I may be so bold. It is my enormous good fortune to have the opportunity today to write to you, and if the marks on the page are not my own, you will know that the words are, and that they are full in earnest.

Oh, that's lovely, Tom, Holohan said, his face unclenching. More of it, boy.

I write to you in the hope, Margaret, as desperate as it may be, that you will consider a path west from your present situation in Boston and come join me here in the most prosperous town to be found upon the high plateau.

Upon the fucken what?

Mountain, Pat.

He finished the beer and signalled for a shot. Slapped it as it landed. He spun the pencil urbanely in his hand—

How's the health, Patrick?

Holohan considered the dreary slopes of himself and jawed on his bottom lip and laid a hand to his swollen gut—

Jesus, he said.

Tom Rourke put pencil to the page again—

My object, Margaret, is matrimony, and I wish to state here that I am in as hale and eager a condition as any man might be, at least given the usual reverses a hard working life can bestow.

He had it within himself to help others. He made no more than his dope and drink money from it. He had helped to marry off some wretched cases already. The halt and the lame, the mute and the hare-lipped, the wall-eyed men who heard voices in the night—they could all be brought up nicely enough against the white field of the page. Discretion, imagination and the careful edit were all that were required.

Do you think she might come, Tom?

Every possibility.

But do you think she'll know what kind I am?

Hard to from a few letters. She might know enough to chance it. We just have to make sure you come across as genuine and not out for the one thing only.

Holohan blushed like a boy and drank up his beer. He signalled to the keep and a brace of shots appeared. The men slapped them and considered first wordlessly and then with a sense of growing warmth their ludicrous situation.

———

On Galena Street he walked the stations of the cross again. The lamps burned a mournful electric yellow above the drifting crowd and the girls of the line cribs called out in brash and intricate detail the index of their arrangements. They did so in seven languages. It had grown still colder and their words rang high on the brittle air. Tom Rourke picked his way along the street avoiding the muddier stretches in favour of his tan Colchester boots. He was this season denying himself the bodily release of the cribs and he ignored with a disdain almost priestly the flashing thighs and moaning lips of the commerce. He was anyhow distracted again on the nerves front. Crossing onto Broadway he carried that weight of weird knowledge or clairvoyance. There was the whisper of a foretelling but he could not make out the words of it. He believed in messages, signs, uncanny harbingers, and as he passed by the Southern Hotel the supper room lights sputtered and went dark and then flicked to life again, as if the joint was winking at him.

There was no fucking way he was going out tonight. He looked in briefly at the Pay Day but only for a straightener. He stood at the brass rail and was consoled by his boots, which were cut stylishly to the ankle length. He engaged a small whiskey and judiciously let it down with a splash of water. He thought fuck it and took to the bar mirrors again for a quiet inspection—

He wore the felt slouch hat at a wistful angle and the reefer jacket of mossgreen tweed and a black canvas shirt and in his eyes dimly gleaming the lyric poetry of an early grave and he was satisfied with the inspection.

He felt for the Barlow jackknife of teardrop handle in the one pocket and for his dope tin in the other and was reassured.

All he wanted from life was quiet and stillness. There was hope of neither in this place. The pit shifts changed and the night heaved and the Pay Day shouldered its way to a condition of full abandon but Tom Rourke huddled into his thin frame at the bar and he was set apart from the hoarse and laughing crowd. He was at a distance of artistic remove from it was what he felt.

He looked in at the Collar & Elbow and sold an eighth of dope to Jeremiah The Chin Murphy there. He looked in at the Graveyard and slapped a shot with Danny the Dog-Boy who was dying of the chest, it was confided, though Dog-Boy had by now been some-and-twenty years in the dying. He was halfways down a glass of strong brown German beer at the Alley Cat and think-ing about death and the poetic impulse in youth when he was informed that he was no longer tolerated on the premises on account of misdemeanours incalculable and here once more was a miscarriage of fucking justice.

———

He walked now on Granite Street—the stations—and the boards of the shanties moaned and creaked in the mountain night and you could not blame them. Even in the present moment there was a great hauntedness to it all. The city was only this short while confected but it was already strung with a legion of ghosts and Tom Rourke could make them out among the rooftops and he saluted them.

———

Midnight kind of direction he had his knife taken off him by a volcanic Mancunian named Shovel Burgess at the Big Stope bar and he took a blow to the nose which bled theatrically. Next he was turned away by a Celestial from a smoky roost of the Chicken Flats on account of dope money that was owed and had been spent instead on tan Colchester boots. He took a smoke of what meagre dope he had left in supply in a backroom full of gleaming Portuguesers on Nanny Goat Hill and he experienced the truth and glory of God the Almighty in the here and now of the opiate night.

———

Once he had a zealot belief that love would save him but now he had doubts. He didn't even know of her existence yet, never mind that she was off the train already, had left the supper room at the Southern Hotel, and was established in a fresh new house on the uptown reaches.

———

He looked in at the Board of Trade again. He took a slow recuperative bottle of stout. He was dissatisfied with the ambience. Too many Irish. There were by now ten thousand Hibernian to the town and they had the place fucking destroyed. A fellow Corkman drinking at his westerly elbow leaned in with an accent from the rim of Bantry originally—

Hear about Two-Bit Billy?

Shot his own toes off, Tom Rourke recited, at the Alley Cat bar.

Not the way I heard it. Happen at the Big Stope. I seen eye witnesses describin. Two-Bit barred out of the Alley Cat since March. Mostly he been drinkin with the Finns down the Helsinki bar.

When did that all start?

March! They was drinkin for Saint Urho. The cunt what chase the grasshoppers out of Finland.

Two-Bit fell in?

Two-Bit fell in. Man's companionable.

And where the grasshoppers head to?

We're gettin off the track of it, boy. The right or the left toes the way you heard it?

Does it matter, friend?

All I'm sayin is you're a honest workin man stood there tryin to have a peaceful drink and there's toes all over the fucken floor? That's lettin the place down something shocken and I don't care what bar.

———

He looked in at the Southern Hotel. He looked in at the Cesspool. He gave a broad berth to the Bucket of Blood which was for newspapermen and touristic types only was his opinion. He denied himself once more the line cribs though he considered briefly a proposal of marriage to Greta of Bavaria at the Black Feather. It was three in the morning. He drank and smoked and moved his feet. Then the black haze descended. Then the music all stopped. Then he felt himself aloft suddenly. He was at an elevation. He was upon the fucking air. He was carried from the Open-All-Night and deposited arsewards to the street. He crawled the breadth of the street on his fours. There was little dignity to it. He rose with grave uncertainty and stumbled away into the night and he carried yet the great burden of youth.

—

He lost his faith in God again around half four in the morning. Now he believed in everything else instead. He believed in spells and enchantments. He believed for sure he could put a spell on the horse. He clamped one eye shut to keep her in focus but she danced about madly before him. A nervous animal, of golden aura, it was mostly palomino in her. She kicked at the frozen hard ground and a petulance of tiny stars flew up in sparks.

Ah go handy, he said, wouldn't you? My head is fucken openin here.

The moon was near and pale at three-quarters. It showed over the East Ridge wanly. There was a witching in its blue milky light. The horse kicked and whined and her eyes flared with violence—

No call for that business, he said.

He tried to get on his feet for the stance of authority but failed it and slid the wall of some old shanty onto the bone of his butt again. Jesus Christ, the cold would go through you these nights. He looked up at the horse and the horse looked down at him. She was beautiful and high-bred and her every muscle shone—

Who the fuck's are you anyhow? he said.

The horse quieted at this and relaxed her head to the one side and stared at him as if she was certain now that she had seen him before but couldn't place him.

Tom Rourke, he said.

The horse stilled herself utterly and fixed the lashes of the long stare on him and he was bound. There was a wretched pain in her someplace.

He rose and wavered on woozy legs. He was operated by an inept puppeteer. He opened a hand to the horse. She flinched a little and stepped back but only by a few dancing steps. He was flirting with her now. He felt he might need a horse one day soon. She lowered her stare again and he put a hand before her face and he felt the hot sick breath on his palm and he locked onto the lash-wide stare.

Closer, he said, and he began tunelessly to sing, working out the words of it as he went—

> *Oh palomino palomino*
> *Sing a song for me*
> *Oh pal-o-mee sweet pal-o-mino*
> *Nothin comes for free*

And fall, he said.

At that the horse buckled onto her knees as if gunshot and rolled onto her side and onto her spine and kicked at the air and showed her crazy teeth and the pain was no more or at least not so she could feel it.

I'll be seein you, he said.

———

He was on Wyoming Street again in the pre-dawn dim. He was a bit drunk still and pretending not to be. He was also a little high. His member was somewhat on fire. The rooftops of Dublin Gulch leaned into each other as though to confide. The gallows frames above the pits were the mountain sentinels and these were elegant, he felt. The prospect of death was a glamorous comfort but it did not hold for long—*oh this brick and mud Calvary my Wyoming Street.* All around him now the inanimate enlivened. There were faces recessed in the shanty walls. He was rattled at this hour certainly. He would never go out of an evening no more. But left alone at night he grew afraid of the dark.

Vows, resolutions: he was twenty-nine years to heaven and must never feel this old again.

Breath of dawnsmoke. Park and Broadway. The winter it came slowly west. He spoke to God again as he stood at that section and looked down on the world—can we see him there yet?

He told God that he was very proud of Him.

The calamity that was Tom Rourke proceeded to Quartz and Main. Despite it all his words tumbled forth and ran freely. Put them to fucken profit, why don't you? He worked up a chorus for a new song about the Orphan Girl pit—

> *Workin down the Orphan*
> *All the hours I get*

> *Girls up on Galena*
> *Got me drownin in debt*

He was in his own right a great scholar of debt. He owed for dope to Bud McIntyre the mock Celestial; he owed for dope also to the true-born Celestials; he owed on tabs at the Board of Trade, the Southern Hotel, the Open-All-Night, the Pay Day and the Alley Cat; he owed on his room at the Zagreb Boarding House, with awesome arrears. He would not live among his own kind. The Irish bastards were sentimental pigfuckers to a man. The Croats knew at least they were bound for hell and they had a knacky way with boot leather.

Ghosts of the night shift drifted by.

The pithead bells rang out.

The girls from the crib windows cried gaily yet and waved.

Vows, resolutions: no more the bottle, no more the pipe, and no more the rips of Galena Street.

Estuarine was a word that could be used. As for a salty tang on the air. The tip of his tongue moved and she responded with a hot switching movement, as of a small bird trapped. Though locked in place between the clasp and clenching of her thighs, and subjugated purely to his task, he felt light-headed and fleet—he felt actually that he was flowing. *Riverine* was also a word, and lovely— the slow meander of it. Greta's scent teased the air and Tom Rourke lay at the foot of a crib in the Black Feather and lapped diligently in . . .

The salty reed beds of her love?

Jesus Christ there was no stopping him when he got going.

The sea field of her love?

Better again.

Tom, she said, you go much too fast today. You have some troubles now, I think?

He ignored the interruption. He pressed on with diligence. It was better anyhow not to speak. The girls made more of you that way. Silence and manliness equated. He had sworn himself against words. Above him Greta writhed now and encouragingly cooed. Put her on the fucken stage altogether. She twisted a slender Bavarian thigh and locked it tightly around his jaw and squeezed and upwards he gazed with mild dismay across the lid of her cunt.

You have me choked, he said.

And you pay for it, she said.

————

A familiar of the premises he was allowed afterwards to linger. He felt clean and honest in the wake of his selfless lovemaking. For weeks now he had denied himself the proletarian release of climax. It was better to keep that stuff tamped down was his new line of thinking. The power of denial gave vigour and erotic glow. The painful heat in his groin was good heat, was good pain. It would feed strength to him naturally as it built up. It would give him bass tones and bottom. He had not come in six weeks bar a lone nocturnal emission beyond his responsibility. He had dreamt of a green-eyed woman from Adrigole. He hated to be wistful for home. He hated the sentimental bastards singing through the streets of the small hours about the hellholes that had vomited them out.

The fine blonde hairs on Greta's forearm were lovely as she arranged the long pipe. He set the dope tin down pleasantly. She unhooked the scratcher and applied it to the ball of dope. She lit a long taper and put it to the bowl of the pipe and heated it and raising himself onto an elbow Tom Rourke drew deeply into his lungs the beautiful chaudul. He glazed into the good light. He saw himself there as he exhaled. Very handsome when high. Face on him like a tortured saint. He watched as

Greta repeated the steps and took her own fill. A tear rolled down his cheekbone sweetly—

Will you marry me? he said.

Greta laughed quietly as she drifted slowly backwards into the stretch and waking arms of the cot.

I'm not the one for you, Tom, she said.

———

Through the haze of bloodshot eyes he aimed for the M&M on North Main Street. There was something honest and reasonable about an eating house at half seven in the morning. There was something maternal and forgiving somehow. We are after coming through another one alive so to speak. He pushed through the doors of the place. Taint of rank bacon, sweat, smoke—

Good mornin?

A half-dozen sets of shoulders groaned from the high stools. He joined their number and took a load-bearing glance from Fat Con Sullivan beyond the counter—

Were you on Galena Street, Tom?

I was not.

You've the waft of it all the same, boy. Mercury Street?

Nor there.

The great Sullivan belly slid the counter like some

class of pup seal and arranged itself complacently. In a
damp whisper—

Did you walk the line, Rourke?

Indeed and I did fucken not.

A tin mug was poured to fill with the purgatorial coffee of the house. He sugared it heavily and blew on its
surface. What the fuck was a sea field? Sullivan plated
up a mess of fried eggs and set them before him with a
mime of delicate care, as if fearful of disturbing a cus-
tomer's equilibrium. Tom Rourke salted the eggs unam-
biguously. He tried to ignore the feeling that he was
being watched in the room. A handful of hard rain was
flung against the window and now he felt the strangest
thing, a thought almost beyond words, that the winter
would have purpose for him yet.

Fat Con was in his realm and glory. He paraded the
counter at the M&M in sacramental mode. He bestowed
forgiveness with his greasy plates. He lacked only the
thurible. He leaned in again to confer—

How's that old London boy treatin you?

It's a job, Con.

He let you work the camera box at all?

Sometimes.

An' he's puttin money in your pocket?

The odd time.

Ye're doin business then?

There's a few coming into us.

But is he right in the head, do you think?

There's none of us great in the rack around here, Con.

The eggs went down controversially. The coffee began to straighten the affair. He rolled a smoke to find the hands were passable steady by this stage. Once more and gauntly he considered his situation. He wrote songs for the bars and letters for the lonesome. He was assistant to the photographer Lonegan Crane, a lunatic, of Leytonstone, East London, originally. His days had been passing with no weight to them but he knew now that fate would soon arrest him. He may have moaned a little at this but such moans were not unknown in the M&M at that hour of the morning.

Con Sullivan laid his belly to the counter again. It was a separate entity almost. You could give its own name to it and put it on a leash. The counterman spoke discreetly now—

Was it yourself arranged the wife for Harrington?

Which Harrington?

Long Ant'ny, the captain.

Anaconda company?

Same.

Didn't know he took a wife even.

Reports are circulatin. A girleen out of Chicago hey. Tom Rourke will be the last poor Irishman without a legal lay to his name.

———

He walked on Main Street in the rawness of its changing weather. There was snow on the mountains already. There was the feeling of All Souls. A familiar from home lurched into the light—Ned Sheedy, of Allihies, County Cork, a miner of the Lexington pit, and of perpetually startled mien. Sheedy dropped his workpail to the ground, hoicked loudly to resituate an amount of phlegm, and leaned in to whisper—

Clearin six dollar a day and I still got the devil in me bollocks.

This is the way, Ned.

The miner jerked a thumb to the Galena Street cribs—

They have me a slave to the fucken gowl in that place.

Ah I know it, boy.

Sheedy's face had an oddness to its set that gave away the buried charge of epilepsy. If the lungs didn't get him the shaking would. Now he took Tom Rourke's hand in his and examined it like a palmister—

Can't see the work in it, Tom, he said. See more in a little priest's.

He picked up the pail to move on but hesitated—

Tormented by fucken gowl, he said. Were we as well off when we didn't have the price of it?

Do you want me to write a letter for you, Ned?

Well, the miner said, and looked away to the mountain wall east, as though spiritual advisors were in seat there.

On the chance of a wife, I mean.

Would you do that for me, Tom?

Look in at the Board of Trade some evening. Five-ish.

———

There wasn't time even for the shallows of sleep. He changed his clothes and paced his room at the Zagreb. He caught himself at passing glance in the shaving mirror. He turned it bitterly to the wall. The pale unlined face was too boyish yet. The sea-blue eyes were too moist and pastoral-looking. He was fucking harmless was what it was. So he opened the razor and laid it to his wrist. He felt the good weight of it there. He was in full earnest. From the dining room below came the murmur of Croat voices and the waft of pigs' toes in their rendered fat—were these now the last of his senses? The razor would deny all destiny. There would be too much pain in his destiny to bear—he knew this already. It was to be read in the white aching of the sky beyond his tiny window. But as quickly as the thought had come he folded the razor again with care and stored it neatly and he was sorrowful—

Because what kind of a fucking Irishman can't even do away with himself?

The loose board's creaking on the stair announced Mama Horvat's approach. The house demon was loose and agile. She was in the room without knocking—

How long more? she said.

I understand that your patience runs short, Mama.

I think you must go now.

But are you not lookin out at it? The winter's in on top of us.

What can you give me?

My word and honour, Mama.

She backed him into the room. She was not five foot

tall but there was a great inhuman force in the palm she set to his chest. She flattened him against the wall—

Dollars, she said.

He owed more than seventy-five dollars on the room. It was a few weak strides of a doper long and the breadth of an uneasy dream. He wriggled from her grasp. She watched hard-faced as he foostered among his effects.

I know that I'm a maggot, he said, and I know that you've indulged me greatly.

He knew also that Mama Horvat had sold a brother of hers and not long ago neither. The brother was soft-headed but even so. To traders from Vancouver the brother was sold. Tom Rourke searched through the pockets of stale apparel and put together eight dollars and change.

One more week, she said.

Thank you, Mama, he said.

Now I am the mama of fucking poorhouse, she said.

———

Next to be endured was the Lonegan Crane photographic studio, the place by daylight of his work and sufferance—

Of course you realise the Frenchies do it peculiar?

How so, Mr. Crane?

They're like the dogs in the street, Tom. The lady's faced to the rising sun and Frenchie's in behind. He's giving it what-for. Hell's bells to buggery, him with his little tongue wagglin' and him with his green teeth? He's biting at the lady's ears! Bang bang bang and the eyes roll up in Frenchie's head!

Lon Crane let the curtains fall on his dark enclosure to obscure from his plates the morning rays.

Oh it's a Godless business, Tom, in the Frenchie style.

The old English staggered to his resting corner. There were flavours of gin and diseases involving stones as he passed by.

Now we know for sure the Montrealers is the worst of the Frenchies, he said. Oh by far. They're ugly and they suffer from lungs. I'll concede some of the ladies is pretty but not so you'd notice, not with them and their little faces rammed into the pillows and here comes Frenchie! Barrellin' in southwards!

He collapsed to the wingback chair shipped in special from the Isle of Dogs and Tom Rourke counted off the beats of the morning ritual. It was akin to music. The spectre of Alrick Dusseau would appear now in Lonnie Crane's range, the general sin of Frenchness submitting to the particular—

What the Monsieur Dusseau studio has in mind, Tom? With his new line of portraits, so-called? With his back-to-fronts? It's the Frenchie style of fornication, in't it? Sewer of a mind, I say! Ladies looking over their shoulders and staring all gawpy-eyed into the camera? Evenin' wear and shy little glances? Who they expectin' to come visit from that unnatural quarter? Frenchie, that's who! Oh the French rut is precisely what Mssr Dusseau is alludin' to with his filthy bloody back-to-fronts! It's a nod and a wink! It's buggery and cavortion! It's the beasts of the fields!

Dusseau of Montreal was the city's leading photographer. Almost daily Tom Rourke was sent by his employer to survey the Dusseau premises and gauge its state of business. It was in fanatic health. Its fine double-fronted windows on Granite Street displayed the likenesses of miners, barkeeps, labourers, of cooks and maids, Poles and Irish, Croats and Cornish, of newly-wed couples in formal clinches, soon enough of their ghostly offspring, and laughing cats and queenly dogs, and lately, after this new and salacious fashion, the portraits of ladies but indeed posed back-to-front, gazing coyly over their shoulders, showing in evening gowns the bared knit blades, the length of neck, the fall of loosened hair,

with the profile turned just so for the line of nose, and
the tapering of waist, and suggested, just out of frame,
the swell of posterior and the one true street of the new
world.

———

The back-to-fronties, Lon Crane said, are an insult to
the God-fearin' order. But we've to go with the style of it
now, don't we? We have no choice, Tom! Mssr Dusseau
has dragged this town into the gutter! And considerin'
where we started the fuck out from?

Beyond, on Broadway, the morning was starkly lit
under a migraine-white and vast opening sky. There was
the barking of the yard dogs and the cries and hollering
of the horses and men. Lon Crane listened, too, and he
took it all in—

October? he said. Give you the bloody morbs.

He rose from the wingback and made for his desk.

Opportunity, he said, has a way of gettin' the fuck
away from me.

He consulted his ledger, and sighed—

We do have a booking, Thomas. One o'clock. Matrimonial.

———

And the bell trembled yet on its one o'clock toll when Captain Anthony Harrington of the Anaconda company appeared at the Crane studio with his new wife in tow. Harrington was lean and tall and cable-wiry. Hard flint eyes. A seabird feeling. A heron, or a cormorant, Tom Rourke saw him as. But there was no cruelty there. He was afraid to touch the wife. The wife was slight and inclined for the shadows. If she could seep into the walls of the place she might do. Harrington tried to help with the removal of her coat but she sulked his hands away. She was not quite beautiful or not exactly so, and she was by no means young. Easily she was thirty. She was fair, complexion delicate. A slight crook to the nose. Eyes of wren's-egg blue and one inclined to say hello to the other but not unattractively. There were ramifications in her eyes. Lonnie Crane circled and fussed madly about his clients—

And how've you found the town, ma'am?

It's a lot to take in, she said.

Her voice was small but not uncertain.

The hope is, Mrs. Harrington, that we've become more civilise' in ourselves round the edges. That right, Captain?

Will this take long? Harrington said.

———

Tom Rourke unrolled the backdrop of sky-blue. Its soft-ness against the sharp mountain light was intended to take the look of sickness off people. The couple was arranged in its pose. Harrington squinted a slow enquir-ing look at Rourke—

Berehaven? he said.

The far side of it, Cap.

Ah yeah.

The captain stood with his arm placed torturously around his wife's tiny waist. It was clear that every ounce of her resisted him.

The camera was introduced. The process was ex-plained. The couple was eager to be gone. Tom Rourke strained for her eye. She sensed him but denied it. There was something gamey though. Yes there was a rascal set to her jaw. She did not speak but he could hear clearly what she was thinking—

Be wary.

A single heated flash. The marriage portrait was com-pleted. Harrington shuffled his weight one foot to the other and took some colour to his cheek—

And of the lady alone? he tried.

A back-to-front portrait of Mrs. Harrington was arranged. She removed a light calico shawl and with a small proud thrust showed the neckline of her evening gown. She turned from the men then and looked back over her shoulder and loosened her hair. There were fronds of lace at her fine expressive neck. Her skin was pale and flawless but for a single electrifying mole on the shoulder's blade. The tip of her nose twitched and her eyes searched for the camera but found instead Tom Rourke's, staring—

It was at this moment that his heart turned.

As Harrington settled up with the proprietor, Rourke fetched the bride's coat and presented it and he spoke lowly, averting his eyes—

My regards and congratulations to you, Mrs. Harrington.

She turned to him as she went, and in a hissed whisper—

My name, she said, is Polly Gillespie.

———

He walked on Mercury Street in the cold smoky air. The sky was darkening. He was premonitory again. He let a new song come on the feeling of it. It was set to polka time—

If I had Polly in the woods
I'd do her all the good I could
If I had Polly in the woods
I'd keep her there 'til morn-in'

The ridges were cut out against the dark back of sky. The new city hurtled and the pitheads groaned. The cribs already were lit up, the girls to be seen in silhouette in places—

And if I met Polly in the woods . . .

The street was witness to the fresh glowing newness in him. He walked on into faces and shoulders and hats and mouths and sky. He rose up from himself briefly. There was a transcendental element to the motion. He saw himself down there, as he weaved through the evening crowd, his shoulders knit in fresh thrill and obsession, and his lips moving—

And if I met Polly in the woods
I would kiss her if I could
For that's a thing that would do her good
And a cup of tay in the morn-in'.

Polly in the Woods

Yeah so maybe she kind of overdid it on the blood theatricals. She asked about the matter with a lady she knew in Chicago at that time. It was delicate to bring up but they got to talking it through. There were a lot of possibilities it turned out. The lady told about a friend of hers and she had to go all the way out to Wicker Park then and this other lady presented the items. Three dollars a piece she paid out for these spurts of pigs blood that was all fixed up in what looked like sausage casings. They were a neat piece of work. Slip one of those up easy enough but she thought she'd go in for insurance and slipped up a couple. Harrington wasn't groaning and crying up top of her two minutes and she felt one go. When the second one's popped it's about turn the mattress into an abbatoir. Bloods everywhere. Yeah but he was crying when he did it to her even before the blood situation. Like heavy salty tears falling onto her mother-fucking face. That was the first of the weird things was the crying. The blood it just added to those things. Tell you what it was like the Niagara of goddamn blood and tears was how the wedding night went off.

He'd sent his likeness with the letters but she didn't need it when she stepped down from the Union Pacific. That had to be him for sure. The way he was standing there all stiff and staring out like a statue. She could tell a hank of bad luck from better than fifty yards off. She'd seen it plenty of times before. Up close she could tell there was a fear in him too and it was more than just shyness. Like a priest type he seemed all softspoke and grey eyes that were kind of nice really. He didn't even touch her. There was not a handshake and they were in the registry with the town officials and witnesses. The witnesses were sizing her up real careful. She guessed they were friends of Harrington. He wore a suit looked like it was made out of sheet metal and walked like a man with a pain he could tell you all about. She was married to him not an hour after she stepped off that train. He took her to the

Southern Hotel for a supper then. It was like she was sitting in that dining room inside a strange dream one that felt like you'd had it before and the once was plenty. It was just the two of them sat to eat. He spoke so quiet she could hardly make out what he was saying and she had to lean right in to hear and she could tell he was pretty flummoxed by the top of her dress where it dipped. He said he would be a kind and providential husband to her. She said she'd been to Providence one time so happened and his blank look said this was not any kind of dude for wisecracks. He didn't take liquor himself he said but she could have some sherry or wine if she so wished and she took a small glass. They ate mountain trout and fried potatoes. It was pretty good. One point of it the lights fluttered and went dark and in the half second of dark she had intimations of the grave but then the lights came back on again and she was fine. Harrington apologised for the hotel as though he was liable for it on a personal level. She wouldn't say he was the conversationalist type generally and she heard herself filling up the air with all kinds of nonsense. Talking about the first things that came into her head the types of dogs she liked and the flowers she liked. Maybe he took her already for some kind of imbecile or giddy sort. He sat there looking at her like he was after buying the wrong ticket entirely. But he looked at her in the other way too. He had an interest for sure in what was going on down the top of her dress.

———

The house wasn't what you'd call pretty but it was new built and smelled of fresh lumber and it was clean. It was a good climb away up top of the town. He showed her all the cuts and joins of the lumber like she was interested in that and said she could have it painted up any way she liked and make it look nice. It was the newest house she'd ever live in and the rooms were generous in proportion. She felt like a new crown queen right there as a matter of fact and she thought maybe this whole thing is worth the candle after all. His grey eyes they were definitely nice and he surely wasn't fat. But then he started in at the praying.

———

Now it wasn't as if she wasn't expecting some prayerful times after the letters she'd had and in fact all the way over on the train rides she'd taken to get herself across the plains and through the mountains all the while climbing she'd tried to put herself in touch with a spell of Godliness. She really did try hard. Closed her eyes and said His name and asked Him come down and enter her. Said I am climbing right now oh Lord I am climbing into your arms. Go right ahead and enter me blood and veins right now oh Saviour. She was only a sinner no worse than no other. And she explained her entire situation to the Lord right there. That she'd been writing to a suitor out west and hearing back from him and it was clear the man was the God-fearin type to a good extent and she said if that wasn't exactly ideal personality-wise it was gonna be better than the other type. She'd known one or two of the other type. She'd known a few actually. I could tell you some stories Jesus. And the train rolled on and on as if it was on the forever line and picked out the great open fields and the plains and there was oxen sometimes and pigs in wallow and small lonesome towns and crossings and by night especially they were lonesome and there was farmers and rivers great and small and she was coming and going out of sleep and waking and she fell into this whole long very casual type conversation with the Lord. It was dandy. It was like she was talking to a real good friend of hers. She said this suitor gentleman was Irish but sounded as if he was High Irish not no Cabbagetown type. He was a miners boss a captain of the Anaconda company. She liked the word Anaconda the way it rolled out when she was speaking to the Lord. She said she would do right by the man if he would do right by her. I have put aside my skittery ways once and forever Jesus. They would have pretty little children and sit on the porch and watch the setting sun after supper. How would that be? Sun on the mountains in the eveningtime and nothing stronger than black tea going down the hatch. Wouldn't be a bad way for a girl to wind up considering some of the ways it could have winded up. The Lord didn't seem to have much to say in response to all this but the ease of the way she talked to him on that journey out west was like never before and she thought maybe this is what it feels like when Jesus come down and enter you. Just like being with a friend.

———

But this Anthony Harrington was a whole other matter on the Jesus-botherin front. Mean to say he and the Lord were going right at it when he prayed. She could hardly believe it when he got down on the parlour floor that first night on his knees and tied himself off.

She was about her bath supposedly. She was preparing herself supposedly. She wasn't supposed to be looking. But she cracked the door an inch and looked out and he was right there on the floor with a length of rope wrapped around his waist over and over again and with the end of the rope he was whuppin at his own back and praying out loud. It was in the speaking of the tongue way of praying. Crazy words all but strangling the dude at the throat and yeah there was plenty of sobbing too. Big hard gulpy wet sobs. And the whup the whup the whup! He kept it right up and kept it up hard and she said to herself well Polly Gillespie how about this for another good one you just landed yourself in.

Wasn't exactly a mood-setter is the truth of it but from here she guessed they were settling on going to the bed. They were a married couple after all. She went back to her bath and had some dark thoughts about luck and fate and the way the blood could be made to flow and mingle with your own dirty bathwater if things got bad enough. But then she thought fuck it and dried herself off and slipped up the sausage casings. She could stick a situation out was a thing she'd say for herself.

Well he started kissing at her and pecking at her like a nervous old hen as soon as they were in the bedroom and it all went in that particular direction quick enough. She reckoned he'd definitely done it once or twice before but not a lot more than that which was saying something given he was forty-five years old. At least that's what he was passing himself off as but then again she was passing herself as twenty-seven. He was grey about the chest hairs that made it feel like he was old. They were wiry and sprung tight.

She said she was sorry about the amount of blood and mess and tried to imagine a face onto herself like a silk white virgin despoiled at last in some grotto type set-up and harp music is playing why not. He was just kind of sat there by the bedroom window all hangdog and staring out to the uptown reaches and chewing on his long bone jaw. He turned and looked at her then and from the back of his throat made like a gull's sudden cawing noise and it was real loud and shockin and she guessed this was the dude's idea of a joke of some kind. She gathered up the sheets and took them out and put on fresh and one way or another they got through the rest of the night without dying of the embarrassment. She lay mostly without sleeping and anyway the city of Butte it turned out was no kind of sleeping town. This place was screeching and crazy and loud as the depths of hell.

Next day was the photographs. The studio was run by a madman English looked like he just crawl out of a bush ass-first and he kept sputtering some gibberish at her she couldn't make out the half of it. His boy was carrying stuff around and falling over some. Harrington was antsy and strange as if he hadn't got his full measure of praying in and she was all gussied up like a five-dollar turkey. Got the likeness taken as a couple then she got a portrait done and that boy was looking at her so hard it was like he just discover eyes.

He spoke to her at the end and he was another Irish and a doper type and she had a dark feeling all at once like a cloud was passing over and suddenly everything was chilly and there was a real weight to it.

———

Well the days went by. She set to organising the house as if she knew what she was doing. Harrington came at her a little in the bed but not so much and at least it was quick when it happened. The whup the whup the whup. She had run off all her topics of conversation pretty much. They sat mostly without talking in the evenings if he was working days and days if it was nights he worked. It was easy enough in the silence though. After a while she felt he was truly a good man and she could have had worse luck. He didn't do the praying and the rope business right there in front of her but he knew that she knew he needed that. It was like an agreement was worked out between them.

———

Maybe a week had passed and he was working days and she saw the doper boy down outside the house. He was staring up the street like he was stacking up the courage. She didn't know for what reason but she ran straight to the bedroom and painted her lips.

He was at the door then. Stood there with a fancy white card envelope and he said Mrs. Harrington. She said I told you what my name is. Polly, he said, and he had this wicked type smile like he was trying to put some cheek into it. She saw then he wasn't as young as he looked.

He had brought the photographs. In the matrimonial it looked as if she and Harrington had just bought a one-way ticket to the boneyard. Portrait of her alone she was looking kind of moved you could say. The boy said as much too. He told her she looked so real in it and true to life and just one of a kind. But that was the kind of thing Tom Rourke would say to her often.

I think you were looking at me, he said.

Even on that first visit he kissed her a bit. She didn't give and she didn't pull back from it neither. Dark cloud passed over again. That kind of heavy weight feeling. But then he went away again and she thought nothing of it really and she wasn't that worried about it. He was just a boy with a measure more front than he deserved. She didn't think he'd come back again but the very next day he came back.

Is the captain in? he said.

You know that he's not, she said.

And she made to block the door and he pushed in past her and he was squeezing at her kind of but she pushed him right back and they were maybe halfways playing and halfways fighting. Fighting and laughing kind of. And then he was kissing her real hard and before she knew what in the hell was happening she was giving some back and interest.

⎯

But mostly all they'd do in those early times is they'd sit and talk to each other and they could surely talk a lot.

They were both born under Cancer so there was that to get into. He said that in scripture God commanded the Israelites to forego the Canaanite practices of divination including the Zodiac so that was a definite sign it meant something for real if God was coming out against it. He said the age he was at now Saturn's Return was in his sky and that meant a big change was coming in his life you could put your last dollar-fifty on it. It turned out that he was twenty-nine years old and just two years younger than she was and he didn't even look it. He didn't look too strong. He was thin and whippety kind of and he had eyes that were real bright like some elfin creature just crawl out of a forest tale of the olden times. But she liked his voice and clothes and his nutty smile the way it lit up his face all lantern bright.

She told him about herself or some of it. That there was no family. That she was reared at Saint Dominic's and that's not to be taking out the violin for you and it was there she was fixed up with the Scotch name. You definitely don't have a Scotch look, he said. He reckoned she was some kind of Swede actually going by the colouring. She said he could be right and who knows and who cares anyway when all that matters is where you are right now. He said are you happy where you are right now? When you're here I am, she said, and right then she knew that they were falling.

Yeah and she told him she'd got in some trouble back east and he said what kind of trouble and she said oh the capital T kind.

———

The top of the town at that time was only just getting built up and there wasn't many people living there yet but more and more were arriving every day and there were men carrying the lumber and banging it all together and singing these bawdy type songs in what must have been the Irish tongue. Horses and carts and eyes was what she was saying and they knew he couldn't call any more by the light of day. They hadn't done it yet but they'd come close enough. He said she teased him on and maybe she did a little bit. She could feel the power she had over this half-boy half-man. It was nice. He said he would come by night when Harrington was working and she didn't believe it really she thought that was the end of it all and maybe she was sad a bit and maybe she pined a bit when three or four nights passed and he didn't come by but then the next night she heard a stone on the window.

That was the night they did it first. He came whimpering like a little dog for a start and then roaring like a train like a boy who never come in his entire life before.

It wasn't like he was the first doper she ever knew. He said he was swearing off that stuff anyway and that's where he had been these past nights. Getting himself all straighten out for her. He said he was sick still but he had to see her or he'd probably just die.

———

Now a thing you'd say for a doper always is a doper knows the backways of a town and Tom Rourke knew how to get around the city of Butte in those times like no one's business. So they took to going outside together. They started to roam the streets of that town in the dead of night. It was scary and dangerous and they could have got caught at any minute but if you stick to the backways nobody can see you in the shadows and what she liked best in fact was the way they took the risk. Oh and that town was really alive at night in its shady parts. They'd have maybe half a bottle of whiskey or rum which helped a little with his shaking situation and some smokes and they'd just lurk around in the shadows and kiss and fondle each other a bit and walk across the rooftops and watch what was going on in the town with the Celestials and the line girls and the fighters that was of all races and he said I tell you what Polly I'd write a whole book you give me half a chance.

They were always making wisecracks and playing with words and making up nonsense words. He had these long fingers like a piano player and he could make them tip almost held around her waist and he'd do other things with them too. He'd sing his little songs for her that he wrote for the bars for the miners at night they'd pay him with just some drinks and tobacco mostly. He wasn't much of a singer though.

They learned quick enough they could talk to each other without speaking. Like he'd start off a notion in his head and she'd finish it off for him or vice versa and they were never off with the sense of it not even once. She knew she was in a lot of trouble already and she wasn't three weeks in Butte.

Only once before she'd had a friend like that on the telepath level. It was at Saint Dom's with Jed the old Scotch who worked in the gardens there and from when she was eight or nine years old she was his favourite of the girls. She'd help him with the pruning jobs in the yards. They could talk too just by thinking. Like he'd say you see that butterfly there Polly with the pink at its tip and she'd say that's a pretty one and he'd say yeah and it's a rare one too for this weather and not a word would have passed their lips. When Jed went and died of the stomach she thought she might even croak herself. She was fourteen years old and started to run away and all that stuff and climbing up trains and got as far as Providence that one time and Worcester another.

With Tom Rourke it was more than butterflies they were talking about. He'd start off a line about what he was going to do to her and she'd finish it off for him and boy she could really lay into the ruby stuff and he'd blush like a tomato and not a word would have passed their lips. She liked to see him blush like that. He said all kinds of sweet things too. Things that from any other man she'd have run a half mile from and fast. Things like he said that whatever their souls were made of they were made of the same substance. But she believed that then and she believes it still.

Yeah but Harrington was watching her already like a highly educated cat of some type. It was as if she had a high colour up like a fever case and the captain couldn't help wondering about that. He came and sat beside her one day in the window seat he'd built in. The first of the real snow was coming down steady in a moving blur and it made a kind of picture scene of the uptown and somehow it was weird and toylike the way you shake an ornament for snow. He put a hand on hers to get it started and launched into his longest speech of all time or just about. He said he knew it must be hard coming from a big city to a smaller town but this place had fine prospects and was growing all the time with the money they were paying out there were boys didn't have the price of soup back home taking six and seven dollars a day. Also he said there was every chance that soon enough there'd be children to look after if the Lord gave his blessing in that way and maybe she'd find there'd be stimulation enough in that. She was a young woman yet and he knew that a young woman needed stimulation in her life that was understandable. She didn't see any gain in trotting out an answer to that. She just looked out at the snow coming down and felt his hand tighten like a nutcracker on hers. The most important thing, he said, is you don't switch onto the wrong set of tracks.

Same night Tom Rourke came by like a fox in the dark when Harrington was away the pit and she knew he'd been doping again the way that his eyes were pinned and burning like stars. She said hey now listen. She said we got to make a decision and quick. She took his face in her hands and looked into those eyes and hey listen up boy she said this is fucking real.

Now in those times you could strike west along Granite Street and just keep going and find yourself in the edges of the forest pretty quick even on foot and for the first time that night they walked right out of town. It was like they were on a practice run. She knew they were both thinking it without even saying it. What if we kept going? What if we were to run and never once look back?

They were wrapped up in wintercoats but feeling the cold all the same it was a good painful cold that made you truly alive at your personal extremities and the further they climbed into the wood the more the pressure of their situation seemed to ease off. A little river moved up there and ran in silver through the trees and made its own spooky night music. There were ruins of shacks. Old hunting shacks and claim shacks that had never paid out these falldown premises all hanging loose planks jutting out like broken elbows and holes in the roofs. Night birds that were eerie types but she did not know the names of birds in the particular. It was said there was vagrants and runaways up there too but they didn't meet nobody for a while and didn't hear nor see nobody. But somehow they were expecting it and soon enough they saw a lamp burning up ahead in the dark of the night and were drawn to it moth-like even though they were a little bit afraid.

Turn out it was a dude name of Ding Dong. He was so-called on account of he'd been bellhop at the Southern Hotel many a lonesome moon ago was how he put it but had turned silly on account of not sleeping at all and was just not fit for the company of humankind no more. Simple as that. Falling asleep felt to Ding Dong like drowning he said. So he just quit it all and lived in the wood ever since. Didn't sleep nor didn't have to. And there they found him sat outside an old shack he'd fixed up somewhat and tell you what he looked content enough in his way. From the trees he'd hung some old pans that he'd hit with a stick now and again to make a rough percussion out of but he didn't seem all that bad in terms of silly. Not saying you could walk the man into a bank open up an account. But they sat with the dude

Ding Dong an hour or so and passed a bottle around and it was companionable.

He said how he could read messages in the sky and in fires. He said he could have an agitated guess at what was coming down the line for folks. You said agitated? Coz that's how it feels! he cried and slapped his hands together and got all crinkled up laughing. Tell me more she said. And this Ding Dong he said now look it—

There are folks who get certain intimations about what they need to do in their lives. They can feel these intimations like stirrins of the blood but they can't always make sense of them. They just get drawn to acting out in certain crazy ways and boy it's mysterious he said. Feels like they're acting out under the instruction of the moon and tides. It feels like there ain't no plan nor design to it but there surely is you just got to learn how to read it right. But whatever intimation you get about your life you got to follow it through and follow it through and follow it through because elsewise nothins gonna make sense ever again.

I got intimations comin out the ears, she said.

And the dude called Ding Dong he turned to them both all sombre then and he said—

Now look up yonder.

Look up at yonder moon, he said.

You may need to look for a while, he said.

Look real hard.

Fall into it.

Fall into the spell of it.

Now tell me if you can see fires on it?

And there she was with Tom Rourke hand in hand in terrible love in the dead of night and the forest deep looking up to the sky and all at once yessir absolutely they could see fires on the moon.

Now that there's a suretell sign, Ding Dong said, that it's come to a time in your lives you need to act.

And the dude Ding Dong he spoke with this like weird authority.

———

Little river was moving some ice already and long picks of it gleamed like running knives in the dark. They walked on and further on. It was such a clear night and all the stars were out. It was very cold. They sat there together in the wood all huddled up in their coats and shivered and they were miserable in love and they held on to each other for a long time out of the need and they could hear each other breathing.

There is no decision, he said, we've just got to be

together and she didn't have to tell him he was right about that.

We'll put together a stake, he said, and get ourselves to San Francisco and no one will find us out there for sure it's a whole sea of humanity.

They put down their coats then and wrapped up in them and slept like the hallowed dead in the cold cold mountain air.

She reckoned there was maybe an hour 'til the pithead bells were hit. She felt for his hand in the dark and moved him from his sleep and he shook in the dark like a rattle as if he'd just had bleak news out of someplace ominous but he came around then and she squeezed his hand and they rose up together and walked back through the wood. They came to a clearing and sat on a rock for a while and had a smoke and huddled into each other for the heat of it and they could see right down over the city of Butte—

It was laid out flat pan beneath them like some kind of uneasy beast. The echoes of it ran out and shot. Lamps burned against the last of the dark. Tiny voices were floating about in the far distance. There was horses and machines. She knew without it being said that Tom

Rourke was still thinking about fires. He turned to her on the fall of that thought exactly—

Fires, he said.

It's always been a town of fires, he said.

Yeah in Butte there were places had barely been roofed in against the sky before they went up in flames again. Pyro from the Greek, he said, meaning fire and that right there is just one hell of a pyro town. There are some places that just draw fires. Places where fires get up all the time unexplained. So how about he was going to burn out the Zagreb was the plan?

She listened to him talk it all through and tried to make sense of it. He was fixin to make off with the Mama Horvat cash. He knew where it was kept and would set the fire as diversion. Before the smoke even clears we'll be at Pocatello Junction, he said, and the best part of a quarter ways to the city on the bay and they'll think that money it's just gone up in flames.

———

It didn't feel like all that well worked out of a plan to her. She wasn't sure he was thinking straight. Also the way his voice would change up was a concern. The way his accent would change. It was like he was trying on new versions of himself all the time as if they was jackets. Sometimes when he looked at her she sensed again the dark cloud overhead and the heavy feeling. She fixed up a plate of breakfast for Harrington. The light that come through the morning window was grey and begrudging of itself. The long hard season was settling in real fast. She listened as her old husband washed up out back of the house and splashed the cold water and moaned the name of the Lord over and over again and she knew that a heel turn in her life was coming.

There was the deep body pain in his eyes when he sat down to the eggs and links. You didn't have to get up, he said. She said she was hardly sleeping much anyway and they looked out together and a new drift of snow was falling on the uptown like a dirty white mood.

It'll change, he said, when the children come.

When he'd finished he put away the dishes and said I want you to come back to the bed now.

He wept again when he was up top of her by way of adornment to the experience.

The pit is a hard life, he said after. Did you know Tom Rourke was put down the pit when he came over here first? He lasted three hours.

That night when he came up the house after dark scrabbling through the shade of the hour like a furtive elf he opened back his jacket and shirt and showed her with great excitement a fresh scabbed mark on his breast over the heart where he'd carved with the tip of a knife the letter P.

Yeah so the motherfucker was crazy and moonshot and out of control and she loved him even more and so much she could fucking die in fact.

Inside a week from then he had indeed set fire to the Zagreb Boarding House and made off with an amount of Horvat capital summing almost six hundred dollars cash money and with the few belongings and supplies they could manage in a saddlepack and maybe no more than a few hours until it all got figured out they were in the same dark wood on the edge of town with a stolen palomino and he was trying to talk reason and a spirit of co-operation into the horse and it was only at great stubborn length and with dawn already greying the edges of the scene that the horse obliged and they lit out.

Three

Providence

Ah come on to sweet fuck now?

What's it?

I don't want to say it, Poll.

Say it.

I think we're after gettin turned round.

Aw how the fuck, Tom?

I mean where's it the sun's comin from?

What you mean the goddamn sun?

In terms of direction-wise?

There ain't no sun, boy.

I can see that.

It's just . . . a murk.

The murk is what has me worried.

We don't know which way we're headed is what we're sayin right now?

It is, yeah.

A thick grey mist prevailed from the mountains. They rode in the cold rawness of the winter's day and through the extremities of their fear. They were made giddy by the fear sometimes. They were almost singing with it. He pulled up the horse after another short and aimless stretch and dismounted with a townboy's uncertainty to him and helped her down after.

They turned slowly on their heels all around and scanned the country. She gave him a particular look and couldn't help it. They could get no purchase on the geography. It was so cold their teeth whined.

Jesus Christ, Polly.

The panic ain't gettin us no place.

I'm not panicking. I'm just sayin . . .

I think there's more light. Over that way?

Like a radiance . . .

Radiance my ass.

Which'd mean west. How long we been gone?

Six hours or seven. But hey Tom? I got to say it now. This ain't got the makins of a plan.

———

He took her in his arms and held her. She took off her gloves and with her numb fingertips stroked his face and forgave him. He drew a thumb along the line of her cheekbone and the horse leaned in as though a sideman or confrère. The hooktip of her nose was cold and blue as a berry and he kissed it. She put her hands around his back and held him tighter. The hard stabs of his breathing slowed in response. The edge of the forest here felt fated in the way of a final place and this thrilled her to an unholy degree and when she looked up to his eyes again there was a deathloving shine to hers—

Can't you feel it comin down, sweetcake?

Don't say that, Poll.

You think this is it though?

Don't say it . . .

I think this could be it right here.

Don't be drawin it onto us, Polly.

Well it's gonna be it for sure if we're headed back for Butte right now.

That's true.

Coz if we're headed back for Butte?

Oh they'll hang me on the spot.

They rode on again. They rode double mostly. There was no weight to the pair. He got down sometimes and led the horse. He said there was no fear the horse would bake out and she understood without passing remark on it that he didn't know jackshit about horses. He knew a horse by feel, he said. Okay, she said. After a time they heard the mechanics of labour in the far distance and reckoned it was track being laid for the Butte & Pacific and they turned away from that direction in a lively style.

They rode on and passed into a spell of pure quietness like they were alone entirely in the world and as the dark was falling an old claim shack appeared above them set on a ridge as a gift perhaps from some benevolent god that reigned above the November wood and even if its boards and roof were held together on faith alone it was a reprieve from the dank and falling dark and from the godless cold.

He pushed in the door and squinted against the gloom and lit a match and it was doable he felt.

She gathered up some wood as dry as was to be found and lit a fire in the cracked pit and broke up what remained of a settle and fed the fire and it was quickly a friend to them.

He took the short-handle pan from the pack and threw some bacon on it and arranged the pan in the fire and took out the bottle of Powers Special Irish and interrogated the bottle fully by the throat and offered it—

Well, I could use it, she said.

They all but cleared the bottle right there out of nerves and general agitation of spirit. The fear eased off a little. The bacon waft made the place homely. There was as much sky in the shack as roof and this gave the enterprise truly an outlaw feel to it—

All right, she said.

We're livin it now, he said.

They ate quick and listened hard but there was nothing to be heard beyond the contented sounds of the horse as it consorted with its own settling mood outside and the breeze through the ponderosa pine. They drank off the last of the whiskey to no great effect as regards drunkenness. They'd brought two bottles and it was agreed they'd hold on to the other for future situations. They rolled smokes. They got in close to each other.

If we die tonight?

Don't say it, Polly.

But if we die tonight I wouldn't even care one way or the other.

I feel much the same way about it.

She went outside and walked a slow circle around the shack and listened. There was nothing to be heard of men or horses in the approach of any direction. There were no stars for no searchers to steer by. He called her back inside with need. The shack glowed in the firelight. They lay down and wrapped up and could not sleep for terror and excitement.

Do you believe in God the Almighty?

No but I'm in discussions with Him.

I know that feelin.

I think He's close sometimes and other times not a whisper.

Times I've talked to Him easiest been when I'm lonely.

That been oftentime?

Been sometimes. Today I prayed a bit being honest with you.

What caused it?

On account of feelin bad.

About Long Ant'ny?

It's hard to think about it I guess.

I feel bad about the Croats. They were kind to me sometimes.

We're gonna burn in the fires of hell, Tom Rourke.

There's no doubt to it.

They kissed and ran their limbs together. He took off her red wool socks and warmed her toes on his chest. The fire as it burned down and their bodies engaged beneath the wintercoats kept the cold off just about. The fear eased some more. The wind among the pines came now in soft applause as though in recognition of the escapade. In the shack the last of the fire weakened in the grate and in its embers lay an unread message spelled out in a dim glow.

Did you ever hear of the French rut, Polly?

That's gonna cost you extra.

There was nothing out there. There was nothing to grasp on to. The scrub of the clearances, the early snow, the dark hollows among the pines—that was all. He stood in the broken doorway of the shack. The morning was stark in fierce sunlight. He could not place himself here. The horse in union sympathy edged sidelong to come nearer and closed its eyes against the sun and sighed in a great sadness. Snowmelt dripped from the trees. There was running water nearby. He turned from the doorway and looked back at her and she moved at his glance but still she was sleeping. The remnant of a morning dream stirred her bottom lip as if she fumbled for a lost word or the beginnings of a prayer—

In fact in the shallows of sleep she wandered the streets of her old towns again. The streets ran into the wrong streets in the amalgam place of her dream. Voices called out to her. Used the names that once she had used. She woke now with a startle and shot up fast and said—

Well okay!

And they smiled at each other. The clear light of day was a kind of forgiveness. They packed up quickly and hardly spoke at all. There was no need to eat just yet. They remade the fire to brew coffee. They rolled smokes and drank the coffee. They struck off on an old path beaten down who knows when through the clearances and now by the sun they knew for sure which way they were headed.

Already he swung down from the horse in a more practised way and with a little swagger to it even. He climbed from the path to a rock outcrop and took to his haunches and listened all owlish of expression and scanned the distant skies and nodded sagely. You'd give the boy a gold star for the performance, she'd say that. He climbed down from the outcrop and got back on the horse again and they moved on.

They kept from the edges of the wood. They did not show themselves at all. The old paths persisted all the way. Once in a clearance they saw wild horses. As they rode southerly the new winter receded. Now the leaves were on fire still in places. Snow came in scatters but the day had warmed and mostly it did not settle.

　　You think there's heathens?

　　Hardly now.

　　But could be?

　　I suppose could be there's Nez Percé. A few.

　　What're they like?

　　There's one in particular I wouldn't like to run into.

　　Why's that?

　　On account of I owe him money, Polly.

In the late morning they made a fire and ate jackcheese and duff and drank coffee. They talked about San Francisco and how that might be. The sky was blue and cloudless above the forest where it showed and had a sense of longing to it now or call it a nameless yearn. They reckoned up the provisions they had brought. It was enough for a few days. The horse would get them as far as Pocatello if they didn't bake it and from there as unknowns they could move by the rail. He massaged the horse's legs with an expert set to his mouth as if he knew what the fuck he was doing. He said he was not sure how long it might take to get to Pocatello exactly. Whether to measure it by days or weeks even. There was sure to be provisions available on the way if they could brave it into one of the smaller towns. They had only to stay ahead of word of themselves.

Maybe the longer 'til we show our faces the better, she said.

Maybe you're right about that.

The day held calm and fine. They rode at a measured pace and were oddly serene by now as if the world and destiny would surely provide. There was a measure of cool resolve to it. Sometimes he walked the horse.

Mostly they rode double. The hatchwork of the trees rolled by as diorama and caused a soft hypnosis that was helpful. You went at the right clip, not too fast, and it was soothing. They fell into forest dreams as they rode. They fell into the clear sky of early winter and dreamed. This was through the forest ground of the Nez Percé they rode. Somewhere in the distance there was a quickness of words on the air. She flicked his ear in warning—you listenin?

Yes there were voices in the trees.

There? But now gone again.

He pulled up the horse and hushed it—

You hearin that?

Oh I'm hearing it.

They dismounted and she tied off the horse to the frostblack stump of a dead tree and they got down on their haunches and put their ears to the ground and it resounded like the tautdrawn skin of a drum and they listened—

There were voices from the gloom of the ponderosa.

Frenchies, he said.

Sound like it ain't English for sure.

Say we get closer?

Chancy but?

But could be they're friendly?

Fuck it?

Let's try it.

———

Their names were Janeaux and Morasse. They were Métis or mixbloods or at least in that line broadly speaking. They had a couple of half-ass fiddles strung with catgut and they played them in a jaunty style. It was a funny evil twanging music and your feet didn't want for stomping. It wasn't like any French you'd heard before when they spoke it or sang it out. It was full of sudden hollers to make you stand up in your boots but then long quiet murmurings down almost to a whisper-tongue. The pair had a pretty natty mountain pirate air about them. Janeaux was wiry and compact like a strong prodigious boy and wore a small hooped gold earring in the left ear and had black, black eyes under a stovepipe hat tipped to a cheeky and defiant lean and long hair and boots of pointed toe and coloured rags for scarves tied about the neck and wrists. Some silver chains. Morasse stood skinny as a pipecleaner more than six feet tall and wore a pair of fine duck pants he was proud of and a fur hat out of the Quebecois reaches and long hair and much of a similar motley to his companion in terms of fanciful rag-scarves and a musical laugh that sounded like a flute of some rudimentary kind and was sounded often. As they played the fiddles Tom Rourke and Polly Gillespie stepped out and danced a couple of mazurkas. Just there in a clearing of the wood—there wasn't anything formal about it. A nice fire, some new friends, and a few bottles went around the circle. Tom Rourke sang some of his words into it, too, some of the old half-rhyme nonsense and roll-call he had on tap—

> Ain't got a dime
> But the sun's gonna shine
> Coz we's all bound for heaven
> On the Cali-for-nee line

By means of gesture and intonation and acting-out, and with what shared words they had between them from all the blended tongues and places they had passed through in their lives, they got to talking the situation through with this fiddle-scraping duo of Utah-bound mixbloods. If each pair was discreet as the other about their true histories and intentions, there was a sympathy here, too, and anyhow it was good manners to share information—

The weather that was coming. Who was it was out in the country just now. The provisions that were available. The range detectives who roamed in search of cattle-stealers and train bandits and reprobates general. The chances of summary execution under the eye of the law or what passed for law in the sundry districts a soul might find itself ghosting through hereabouts. Where there were fair men, and where foul. The fauna, the flora. The mushrooms that brought visions, and those that brought fracas and consternation to the bowel and gut regions.

They conversed (after this make-do style) throughout the slow dusk and into the long night and they shared out their vittels and drink. The company was pleasant, and it must have been getting along past midnight when one of the mixbloods, it might have been Janeaux, but who knows, for it was hard afterwards to recall the precise sequence of events, but one of them produced a good-sized canvas bag and opened its drawstring ties, and on a flat rock in the glow of the firelight spread a fine share of dried fungi, and displayed them with pride and a flourish—the mushrooms seemed almost to breathe—and then he took a handful and set to chewing on them, and one by one they all did the same.

The music continued.

The firelight made it a room.

The drinking stopped as if some ungainsayable ordinance had just now been decreed by judges on high.

After a brief mopesome interlude spent investigating the palms of her hands Polly Gillespie got snagged on a fiddle line and took to her feet again and tried out a dance step that was unusual in style and not like anybody had ever seen before. Her arms flailing banshee-like. Her neck swivelling. Eyes popping like a swamp frog's. Little feet stomping off in this direction. Now that. Hips moving like ooh-la-la. Then she threw up right in the middle of it all.

I don't know if this one'll catch on, Tom Rourke said.

Then the lovers were among the trees and in a dream haze the night rolled out in carbonblack and there were hollows of that wood so dark you'd to shade your eyes against it but if you stared into the darkness long enough there were colours that bled out.

And they spoke into the dark hollows and the hollows in slow echo replied and they fell to their knees in religious awe.

Now they were on their fours among the trees and snuffling about like hogs. Yeah and snow it truly was an incredible substance when you put it to the lips or say you got a little lick of it on the tip of your tongue—like so—and felt the tiny stars explode.

The Frenchie types being by a long measure more familiar with the contents of the canvas bag and the properties thereof just remained sat in the swell of firelight and worked at their half-ass catgut fiddles and occasionally the pipecleaner Morasse would take to hollering out a line or two of a ditty of some kind. By this moonful hour it was a yearning music that wanted for other places, for faraway places, for places nobody had ever been to in actuality but still could feel, and Tom Rourke on his fours a little way off among the trees and crawling about the snow stopped up all of a sudden and listened to the song that was sung and found himself . . . moistened of eye. He hadn't found his own style yet and knew it.

Yeah but anyhow the nightsky was something to write home about and Polly Gillespie lay flat panned out in the snow her four limbs extended like spokes to make a wheel and she looked up and tasted the mineral stars and oh boy it was like a sweetish aniseed taste. Then she was above it all and looking down somehow—

The winter trees were packed together with bunched ferocity.

Jesus' breath was in the dark breeze.

The northern lights made a gliding motion in slow greenish swoops through the sky and she wondered what her mother must have looked like—did they look just the same, with the same little twist of eye?

Tom Rourke meantime stared kinda loosejawed into the flames of the campfire and saw again the great conflagration that had engulfed the Zagreb Boarding House all hallows eve orange and cardinal red and he believed it would have sparked up anyhow as a thing like that was just fated and meant to fucken be and was even a benevolence—in fact—against the drab winter night its colours had so gaily enlivened and hey it gave the motherfuckers something to talk about didn't it. He was entirely guiltless now and free and he opened his eyes and looked up as with a gentle prodding of the bootsole the dude Janeaux aimed him back from the embers of the fire. He had just about crawled in there. There was a beautiful heavenly fragrance. It was of his eyebrows singed.

Oh and the night birds sang and the fiddling worked to string together the branches of the pines and the pines in the sweet-breath-of-Jesus breeze moved and whispered.

Was about this point of it Polly Gillespie found a

dead orphan tree like a blackened stump that offered its lower reaches like a great palm and she sat into it and felt bethroned and right there and then she named herself queen of the forest. Sombrely she informed her beau Tom Rourke of this elevation and he made her a crown. He fixed it together with some twists of ivyvine and fitted some pine cones to it just so and a couple of raven's feathers and arranged it precisely to fit. She paraded the circle of the firelight then wearing haughtily the crown. The mixbloods applauded and bowed.

Next on a sudden hot notion she took her swivel-eyed beau by the hand and they went with pride and discretion to a hidden part of the wood and made love extravagantly. Right there in the snow. Rolling and chuntering. It was the dead of night but the night was charged and voluminous and alive. They didn't even feel the cold on their moonwhite hinds. The lovemaking was raw and animalistic and took them from themselves entirely and they would both confess at a slightly later time that in fact it was a bit much. Under the circumstances. Felt as if they'd rollicked in a butchery.

By the time they got back to the circle of firelight the mixbloods had descended somewhat from the higher plain and were passing a bottle again and now it was pure laments and hard melancholy that issued forth from the catgut fiddles. Remorse too. All the lonesomeness of the world. Tom and Polly made a great cloak of their wintercoats combined and they wrapped up inside of it and listened and were in love. By and by the music was left to die off and the talk resumed, after its own style, and by means of mime-play and sputtered exclamations the pipecleaner Morasse explained the dangers of travelling the high woodland stretches. It was clear from the antic nature of his gesturing and the way his eyes were out on stalks that those dangers were not to be taken lightly.

Tom? You can get turned round is what he's sayin.

And don't we fucken know it sweet-thing hey?

When you lose your sense of direction in the mountain forest, Morasse intimated, then quickly you can lose the grip of yourself entirely. You can lose your mind if it comes to it.

To illustrate this last point he flapped his hands about his head crazily so they were away into the sky like spooked birds and he let his eyes roll up, too, and popped them.

Think I get you, Tom Rourke said.

They had the sense that this wasn't news out of last week the pipecleaner was telling them. That always there were those who had been drawn to the forest deep for the shelter it provided and for the cover it gave but what felt safe as the womb could in fact be a place that would make for a quick ending. Quick as it'd look at you.

And so at length a troubled sleep came and it was full of dreams of foreboding and dark mountains and heavy water. Her dreams slipped into his, and infected them, and his to hers, and the infection was squared. She wore the crown still as she slept and woke with it halfways slid from her head the next morning or in fact it must have been going on for noon. The sun was high above the pine trees. The mixbloods had departed but had left stylishly the last flourish of a silent farewell. A scatter of the magical dried fungi was laid out as a gift on the same flat stone and in the white-grey ashes of the dead fire a design had been drawn with pointed stick or toe of boot—it was a heart shape with an arrow shot through it.

When we get to San Francisco, Tom Rourke said, I'm gettin that inked onto my arm just maybe about . . . here?

A bit higher, she said.

They rode on. They rode double. The day was sharp and bright. They were mellow of mood if not entirely at a distance from the sadnesses natural to both of them, and these they knew were sadnesses unanswerable. She lay her face to the hollow of his back and closed her eyes a while. She felt his chest swell out and knew it was the fact of her embracing that made him proud. The haze-work of the trees drifted past, and the sunlight webbed, and he was trying in his mind's eye to establish himself as the practical type. Among their supplies was a day or two's grain for the horse as far as he could reckon it. There were scatters of aftergrass viable in the clearances. There was water everywhere. He stopped at a sheltered place and he set the horse to feed for a while. Polly Gillespie lay down and wrapped up in the coats and rested.

He stood above her and off to the side. He leaned back against a tree for the angle. He arranged the view of it. He wanted to see it just right, as a tableau—the woman, the horse, the wood. A slant of the winter sun came through the trees to light his face. It felt good. He felt the twitches of a foretelling but they would not settle and fix. He could find no view on any kind of future just yet. He wasn't too worried though. He always felt there had been something wrong with him before that he never had luck in his life but now he had all the luck in the world. It was laid out before him, as a tableau.

The country started to change. They were by now descending. The forest ground was thinning out in places. They aimed back into the thick of it where they could. The old paths persisted all the way. They crossed a drift of snowfields. They followed the course of the falling sun west but at a southern slant—

When we was doing it last night?

I remember it vivid.

It was a horror of the flesh, Tom Rourke.

Not sayin it wasn't.

Felt like we was being watched, too.

Watched how?

Felt like there was eyes.

Wasn't the mixbloods if we could hear the music but?

Ain't sayin it was eyes of humankind.

Okay, Poll.

When the darkness began to fall they took shelter in a deep arbour of Douglas fir and they made a fire quickly. They spread out the food that was left. It was down to a few hanks of cheese and some penitential duff. They ate after this sad and frugal fashion. After a time he took out the dried fungi and they had a good look at them. There was just about a feed each in it.

We keep 'em for special, Polly Gillespie said.

Absolutely.

Say when we make it to the Bay of San Francisco?

Makes all kinds of sense.

Be a way of makin the whole thing I don't know how to say it but?

Like a ritual is what you're saying.

See what rises up from the water out there, you get me?

Oh I do, Poll.

They looked at the fungi another while. It wasn't time for sleep yet by the feeling of things.

Fuck it, he said, and he scooped up a half-share of the mushrooms, and he took to chewing on them, and she did the same with the rest.

They did not move from the circle of the fire for the duration. In the darkness all around there were presences. From the edges of the scene came hisses and whispers and from the distance there were war cries. There was a clap of thunder and again twice like double gunshot. A sudden vaulting silence that was worse. A heavy sulphurous note on the air. A body of water palpable nearby and sinister. It was in a place of old killing they'd settled for the night. By a river of blood or a lake of fire. And now in a flash the sky was lit up and displayed and you might pick a night for dry thunder and fork lightning as campfire spectacle but sweet Jesus Christ not this one please. A flash again and a skyhorse reared up there and a great keening came up from what sounded like a bunch of ancient types screeching it out like motherfuckers and the wind rose and the thundergod clapped and the fuck was the death-like waft hey? It was the rank iron stench of fresh-cut human liver on the air was the fuck what it was. They huddled together and shook like petals in a breeze. They hid beneath their wintercoats. They rattled their bones as skeletons dance. Their eyes popped and their ears were fucking crazy. They shut their eyes tight and the visions worsened. Ten thousand warriors crossed the sky baying and hissing and making throatsong and lightning ripped open the belly of the sky and Tom Rourke at his last tether rose onto his knees with arms and hands flapping wildly in surrender as from the sky's bellywound the attacking hordes descended—

Americans! he cried.

The next morning came up corpse-grey and ominous. Winter by now was truly the sour landlord of the forest. There was bite and needle to the wind and it had grown again colder. They packed up in silence and made off in a sheepish fashion from that district. There was also a defined sense of hurry about them. They crossed a shallow river and went by the banks of a dead lake from which the stumps of ancient trees showed like broken teeth and it was the most haunted place that was ever felt. They talked little and the morning passed by very slowly and the shades of the night lingered—

One point of it, she said, I think I might have met my father.

Put it behind you, he said.

They rode on. They needed provisions with urgency now. They had no map bar the one he talked out of himself while pointing vaguely in westerly and southerly directions. The talk was fooling no one. They came off the trail and stopped a while in a dank hollow that felt like an alcove for the laying out of the dead and they ate the last of the cheese and duff. There was the funereal odour of juniper as in a church incense. The food would not run them for long. The next hours went by on a slow parade. The day never brightened at all. The horse was tiring and he walked it for a long stretch. They were getting hungrier now just by thinking about it. They were free and with full hearts though—there was that—and just then as if directed to the scene by hands unguessable they came upon the man they'd come to know and recall afterwards only as the Reverend.

———

He was sleeping ravenously in a covered wagon of the olden era. His belly rose up to show a filthy undershirt and his snores just about lifted the canvas. The wagon was out of a pioneer tale or much as you'd imagine it. They watched from a short distance among the trees. His belly came up on a rhythm and his snoring whined and sawed at the air. There was a real engine behind it. There were no horses. It had the look of an encampment more than a resting place. Ash heaps hither and there. A rudimentary smoker rigged up for fish and small game. Some clothes on a make-do line—a black suit with a solemn history to it and dirty snow caked into its creases. The snoring juddered and hacked at the air. The man truly had a working set of pipes on him. They watched a while more and sensing their presence at last he shot up on a startle and they saw that he wore a priest collar above the undershirt and there was a great reddish-white aura of unruly hair and somehow they felt okay about it all despite the distress of the undershirt, which was extreme. Hereabouts the feeling was benevolent and maybe they could use a man of the cloth right now was the truth of it.

He seen us?

Oh he seen us.

They climbed down and tied off the horse and approached with friendly gestures and smiles and with something akin to spiritual need in fact. They saw then a fresh burial mound on the far side of the wagon and the benevolent feeling faded off somewhat. The man they'd call the Reverend considered their approach with puffy eyes and took on a high colour as they came closer and clutched at his crazy hair—

Hoodlums of Love! he cried.

Once it got itself on the tracks his speech was unceasing and gruffly certain and it came from the north of England reaches—

I don't recognise the bastard Montana territory, he said, cracking an egg into a tin mug of coffee. Not for one bloody minute do I recognise them Anaconda whoremasters.

Neither I don't recognise the bastard Idaho territory, he said, swirling the mug with a jaunty motion. Is the invention of scoundrels, actually. Is a make-believe and nothin more.

I do most certainly recognise the sacred territory of Our Lord Jesus Christ the One True Apostolic Saviour and Our Thorn-Bled Martyr, he said, swallying the egg-riched coffee whole, and I recognise the miracle of His Virgin Birth in filthy stable when all the angels was left cryin.

With that he began to weep himself, right there by the wagon, right there among the trees.

During the course of his wide and ranging conversation the Reverend climbed into the storied black suit, which brought relief to all parties. He itched at the angry red calluses that distinguished his hands and wrists as sites of extreme suffering. One point he stood up and performed a careful gyration of the abdomen, first clockwise, thrice, and then contrary, same again.

I got rocks in me gut actually, he said. Burden of Belief is what it is. You see I am a zealot man in an heathen land. I am voice of Zion in an epoch of whores and liars and I mean no personal offence, young friends, when I use such terms. As to each their destiny, as to each no fault. Ye wasn't born askin to turn out the way ye has done. But listen up careful now. Coz there's a speculation that's made by men holier and more book-learnéd than I and it's that Belief goes in at the gut level. Understand? Not at brain, at gut. And all that's in us as sinners, why, it acts agin it. You see there are tiny creatures in our guts so small and infinitesimal, in fact, they cannot be seen nor heard even if you was sliced open 'pon surgeon table but they are workin all the time, they are workin like bastards, and there's hundreds and thousands of 'em in there, the tiny buggers, and they're workin round clock on triple-shift just to keep us in the chains of the corporal realm. They want us concentrated in the body and not in the Spirit. You've to fight the canny bastards at every turn even if they are of your own essence.

Worms of concentration wriggled on Tom Rourke's brow as he leant forward and listened; the corners of Polly Gillespie's mouth tightened with some dubiety as she took it all in.

Now I want you each to put an hand to yer stomach bags, the Reverend said, and they did so.

Can't you just feel 'em? he said. Can't you feel the tiny bastards at work in there? In gut interior?

Jesus God, Polly Gillespie said.

Sweet mother of fuck, Tom Rourke said.

Now for ye, the Reverend said, satisfied with his revelation, and with the hard truth of our bodily betrayal.

Gyrations to one side, the primary weapon the Reverend seemed to employ against the infinitesimal and God-denying creatures of the gut interior was a bottle of Tres Sombreros tequila.

The body corporal tries to repel it, he said, burping back a swallow and passing the bottle. But Belief? Once it digs in and gets i'self settled? Oh, why now it's the strength in me! Why now it's the fire and steel!

He smiled broadly. He was covered in the small bites as will afflict a ginger-complected man in the out country. His was a pale skin mottled and pecked-looking. His eyes were glossy on a haul of hard-won Jesus-love. His hair was truly a one-off. The burial mound was at careful length alluded to and shyly questioned by his visitors. The Reverend sighed and nodded, and there was a great sadness evident. He had just the evening previous buried his one true friend of the mortal plane, he confided. This was a dude by the name of Tater.

Tater Collins, he said. He were from Bradford originally. Laid track from here to Tarnation and back. Dug out mines deep as Australasia. Slaughtered cattle by the hundred. And any time of day or night that man'd sit down for ye at table or trough and ate a stoneweight of spuds, buttered or not. Couldn't read nor write nor reckon but there was a man that contained volumes.

He wept again, gently, and took the bottle again, with a murmur of thanks, and swigged from it.

Now there was a most valuable Christian man, he said.

He went sorrowfully to the burial mound and knelt and laid a hand to the belly of the mound.

Tater, I'm sorry, he said. I should have looked out for ye. I should have known soon's we left Saint Louis ye wasn't long for the stations. I'll write yer family or what's left of 'em and I'll tell 'em ye didn't suffer.

He looked up to his visitors again—

Yes I killed the man, he said. I'd no choice in't matter. At one educated glance I could tell he'd been taken over by . . . Luciferian Entities. I looked into his eyes and I saw not my friend Tater's. No indeed. Friend Tater was long gone. What I saw lookin back at me was the eyes of our dark acquaintance. Oh an' it's by the eyes always ye can tell it.

The Reverend rose sharply then and came and clamped Tom Rourke's jaw in his hand and stared deeply into the young man's eyes for a slow and troublesome minute—

Ghost eyes, he concluded. Syphilitic eyes of whore-spawn. Eyes of lustfulness. Eyes of dopefiendery. But there's no devil in you, son.

Thank you, Tom Rourke said.

How'd you kill Tater, sir? Polly tried.

He shared out some food and drink. There were pull-ings of stringy jackrabbit as had been cooked on an inconsistent spitfire and there was plenty more where the Tres Sombreros came from—he kept a good sup-ply of it stacked under his cot. By and by the company became somewhat oiled. The talk took to itself natu-rally. They yakked away like billygoats the three of them and long into the night. There was a great ease to it actu-ally. They talked of God and the Devil. They talked of the heart and the soul and of love's insistences and it should be noted that Polly Gillespie and Tom Rourke were both very moved at certain passages of the talk—the Reverend's words chided and nagged, yes, but they comforted also as they circled the fireside. The lovers leaned in and listened hard, and both of them wept at one stage or other of it, and not by the stray tear or two, and it got to a point where it looked like it was turning into an evening for tears generally. And maybe it was about midnight again—don't let anyone ever tell you there isn't something about the hour—when Polly Gillespie rose onto her knees and looked up to the stars in a great pleading and cried out—

But you could marry us right now, Reverend!

Under the eyes of God! Tom Rourke cried.

Make it proper! she cried.

Goddamn me I'll do it! the Reverend cried.

Their vows were plain and simple and improvised on the spot as they stood above the licks and whispers of the fire. The Reverend joined them at the hands and they swore each to the other forever until death and even beyond it because that was just how they felt about one another. If there was a next life they wanted to be hand in hand in that one too, come what may. The firelight projected their image on the wagon's canvas, with their hands joined and their heads bowed in respect to each other, and the Reverend a crazyhaired shadow beyond them, and seeming to hover there.

The wedding feast consisted of the last of the jackrabbit fixed up with some questionable cornbread and as much Tres Sombreros as you could line your stomach against. The lately interred remains of Tater Collins was silent witness to the matrimony, and to the hearty celebrations

that followed, and it was far gone in the small hours
when his recent spirit came up from the burial mound
and hung above the scene and blessed the lovers' union,
recognising its special intensity but also its most tenu-
ous grip on the face of the earth, recognising that it was
by the nails of the claw this young pair was clinging on.

In the morning they prayed again with the Reverend
and gave thanks and took a single swally each of the
Tres Sombreros as a sedative against the harrowing and
brow-splitting reminder of what it had done to them
over the course of their nuptial night. They were neither of them used to Mexican drinking but intrigued
by it all the same—its sweet congress and carnival air—
despite the trepanation-like skull pain the colourless
spirit had the pronounced tendency to leave in its wake.
The Reverend gave them a sack of grain for the horse—
he had no bloody use for horsefeed no more, he said,
and they knew by now not to pick at it for details. They
waved goodbye to the Reverend and blessed themselves
as they passed by Tater Collins' mound and they rode
on proudly as newmarrieds.

In the last of that day's light they came on a narrower trail heading due south and climbing and they risked it for a while and no one appeared to say boo to the goose and they climbed some more and they chanced upon another domicile. This one was pretty sweetly hid— you'd have to know about it to find it. It was of a more recent construction than their previous shack and more solid about itself generally but it was deserted all the same.

Could be it's a huntsman's place, he said.

He took down with a marked absence of know-how the windowboards and slapped his own nose with one of them as it sprang free and she fell on the ground and just about puddled up laughing.

They entered the shack then and discovered a place of great bounty. There was smokefish and beans stocked up in a wall of tin cans and hardly a crack in the roof. The firepit was intact and chimneyed. There was wood dried in a stack and some kindling even. There were six bottles of French brandy and a couple of dozen of Canada wine and a good thick layer of dust laid over everything just for the reassurance.

If there was a ball of dope laid in, Tom Rourke said, they could have tied a ribbon round the place altogether.

———

They spent the best part of two weeks in the honeymoon shack. Each day when they got up it was decided that this would be the day to move on but somehow as the morning passed and the fire got going and the blood warmed the inclination seemed to ease off again. Maybe he would write her another lovesong instead. Maybe she would work out some new dancesteps. The Canada wine was not so bad if you kept your nose pinched when you were drinking it. There was not a whisper of mankind to be heard. The snow came back after a run of clear fine days and as it fell it made of their little kingdom a perfect silence.

Once there were wolves to be heard at night to break the silence and they stepped outside deep in the brandy and called back to the wolves in the tongue of the mixbloods or at least the few words of it they'd made off with.

Think I'd stay fixed up here forever if I could.

Do you not think we'd tire of each other?

Not too quick. We might talk a bit less the way time goes on.

Do I talk too much is what you're sayin?

Ain't shy with it for a dude.

Do you find you have a problem with that?

Did I say that I had?

Ah, Polly, we never had a fight yet really.

Only in the bed.

Yeah but that's a natural kinda thing.

They named the place Providence. He carved the letters of the word on a board and she burnt out the lettering with embers from the fire and that looked pretty good and he mounted it above the doorframe. They stood back together and admired it. Time was very still now. It was hardly moving at all in fact. He leaned in and stroked her neck. She felt the pulsing of her throat on his fingertips. These were the days of their marriage. She blew into his ear slowly and controlled it and said hey now listen up coz this is the sea. They found a handy place to wash in a creek nearby or at least they splashed the icy water at each other stood up on the bank there half-naked and shrieking and sometimes their laughter can be heard on the air of that place still. Just listen in. Yes on the bank they slapped the blood back into each other's skin and tickled and laughed. And they lay together half the short day by the firepit and talked in whispers and fell into long poetical type silences. They surely didn't tire of looking at each other. This was in the country of the Nez Percé. There were lingerings of old melancholy in the clearances they walked through on constitutionals and these fed the romance with a darkness that felt natural to it. The haunted music of the place pierced the high country air. She fit just right between the crook of his shoulder and the line of his neck. He was in a state of nice agitation where his mind would not stop in its giddy turning and she was excited by the turns that it took. She called them out ahead of the moment. It was like conducting a tuppenny orchestra. She just ran with the flow of it. She raked him with her nails to his chest. She raked him pretty good. In the bed generally they lost what little of restraint they'd ever known and were like wild animals at it. She got fuck knots in her hair. They ate when they were hungry and slept when tired. The days unfolded and the nights and into the kind of peace that neither had ever known before and it was as if it could have gone on forever.

But then late one afternoon just as the light was dying and sending a green mournful glower across the snowbound trees they came up from a heavy sleep together when the door creaked open and a great presence blocked out the greenish light though he was framed by it certainly as if by a strange auric radiation of the Otherworld. The sonofabitch must have been the best part of seven foot tall. Easy. And about half as wide. He looked down and considered the pair and spoke to them but gently—

I'm afraid it's time, my lovers, he said.

Four

Away the Hunters

Stephen Devane, of Glengarriff, County Cork, a careful sheriff of the Butte police, opened the low drawer of his desk and with an air of startled discovery brought up a bottle of Powers Special Irish and two glasses. He set a glass before himself and the other before Anthony Harrington of the Anaconda company but the mine captain scraped the glass slowly back across the desktop with the butt of a judgmental palm. The sheriff shrugged calmly and with all the good nature he could muster. He hated the religious and he hated the politicals. He arranged his face for them pleasantly always. He filled his own glass a rumour shy of the rim, slapped it, and smiled—the fast charge of the whiskey's burn allowed him to the business at hand.

The best part of Thomas Rourke, he said, dribbled down his father's good leg.

Berehaven, Harrington said. The far side of it?

That's him, Devane said. The father's people were respectable. The mother's were the grass of two cows but the father's were decent. The Peg Rourke they called the father. He'd a leg took off him in the Caminches pit before it played out, a hopalong he was left. Make a box accordion sit up and talk to you.

Would the young fella aim back there?

Doubt he'd cross the water again. The mother and father are dead. The brother got anything was to be took. Anyhow since the Caminches went there's nothin back there. The few sheep . . .

Gauntly the captain jawed on the situation, and the sheriff could read him plainly: to be shamed out here was one thing, to be shamed back home would be unthinkable. Devane moved smoothly to distract—

Was it one of yer places he was sent down when he came over?

It was not, Harrington said. Anaconda wouldn't even take a try on the like of that.

The captain rose and crossed the room and looked out to the grey November morning of Granite Street—

He's a doper?

Martyr for it. Not a Celestial in the town he isn't on laughin terms with.

A drunk as well, of course?

Tongue hangin out of his head. And a hoor-botherer. And light with the paw by pure nature.

Jesus Christ forgive me if I get my hands on it.

Ah listen, Cap? You'd be forgave easy enough. He's only a maggot crawlin the face of the town since the day he landed into us.

The colours of vitality were never in surfeit on the face of Long Ant'ny Harrington but now he was bled-out-looking altogether.

What did I do in another life to deserve it?

That's no way to think, Anthony. Maybe you're as well off out of it?

I married the girl. It's under the law. I can't marry another.

There is that, I s'pose.

The poor godfearing fucken eejit, the sheriff thought. Rip up the cert and it's no one's business but his own. The money he's taking in? He could arrange a woman in to look after him no bother. A devout little Portugueser say. Or a nice Catholic French girl with good colouring. There were women out there with the pure Jesus sweating from every pore.

But Long Harrington jawed on it all bitterly and crossed the room again and planted his fists on the sheriff's desk—

What're you going to do for me?

Devane poured a last taste to his glass and slapped it.

Charges are laid, he said. They're plain on the face of things. The fire's a hard proof but he's gone with money and a horse and a man's wife. If he's found, we've him done for.

The search is mounted, it is?

Yeah but it's a stretch of country, Cap, you know? If you wanted to stay hid and you were careful?

But would the runt not lack control of his lip?

That could be true enough.

Would he have let something slip around town?

Oh, I'll be askin, Anthony, believe me.

The sheriff averted his eyes then to raise a delicacy—

Has the lady any people left after her? Back east? Or . . .

She has no one.

Unspoken on the air of the room then, but deafening—

The fuck were you thinking, Long Ant'ny? Marrying off the side of the fucken road? We're supposed to be respectable people now.

It was the hour of remorse at the M&M eating house. A Sunday morning, white and acheful, and a Saturday night head on every poor motherless buck sat up on a high stool, and every last one of them was family to the fat linecook Con Sullivan.

It was the season of lost souls.

The dead were plentiful on the streets of the town.

Who would be the next to join them?

A fine morningtime question to chew over in Butte at that hour of our desperate lives, and the Hibernian brethren bowed their heads to it sombrely. In sympathy with them Fat Con moved like a sweet old ma behind the counter. He cut off the sausage links and the strips of bacon and flung them with artistic expression to the grill. He cut white loaves on the slicer and chopped the liver into neat hanks with a murderer's relish. He was a man in his time. He was alive to his place and task. He swung his great belly from grill to counter and back again and there was grace to it. Dankly his occult coffee simmered and there were canteen pots of tay stewed black as porter. Dead bloodshot eyes sat in a row for him along the high stools and every last set of them was beholden. He rendered the fats and toasted the breads. It was a pale November sky beyond on North Main Street and Con Sullivan cracked his eggs with princely flourishes. He was dainty about his work as a jewelmaker. An icy gust of the wind assaulted the room when some big fool eejit stepped in and left the door wide open for the North Main view. Con Sullivan roared—

Ah bang out the fucken thing wouldn't ya and don't have us slaughtered altogether!

It was Stephen Devane, the sheriff, who stepped back and closed the door gently.

Didn't see it was yourself, Dev.

The nervous laughter from the stools quietened swiftly as Devane stepped along the line and performed an inventory of the livestock—

A disgrace to our poor tragic fucken nation, he said. Every last manjack cunten one of ye.

He leaned over the counter. He hooked a forefinger at Con Sullivan. The cook glided over as though on small wheels.

What'll I fetch up for you, Dev?

Tom Rourke.

Fat Con removed his greasy apron and jerked his head out back. The sheriff dipped beneath the counter's hatch and followed Sullivan through to the scullery for a quiet confer—

Not a whisper of him since Jesus knows, Dev.

He was here Tuesday morning, Con. He lit out with the little guzz-eye on Wednesday night.

Tuesday? Jesus, he might have been. Now you say it.

Dope in the eyes?

Ah well. At the best of times . . .

Where would he knock off to? Have he people in Missoula, they say? Might have a cousin there?

Never heard that now.

Did you not? And ye'd be close enough?

Close? Ah no. I mean he'd be in the place. And for years goin on now, I suppose . . . But half Berehaven do be in the fucken place.

For the warmth of your smile, Con Sull.

Thank you.

What's he been sayin about the Harrington wife?

He been sayin nothin at all. Which might make it serious.

Now for you.

He'd be ribbed about it along the stools of a mornin but he's not comin back with a single line. No aul' guff out of him. Respectful, kind of?

Jesus Christ, I hope it's not fucken love I'm dealin with, Con?

That would be a raw deal.

Would he go home?

Never.

On account of the brother?

The brother's legendary. Who the fuck'd go home to that?

You missed your callin, Con Sull. That's the beak of the law on your lovely big aul' face.

Thank you.

Why's it the Croats he's bunked up with?

Ah look it. Tom Rourke's the sort who'd have no regard for his own people or at least not to give it to say.

Superior little cunteen.

Now.

Would he handle a horse?

Depend on the beast.

Would he last out there?

Depend again.

On?

Hard to say it but.

Go 'head?

Tom Rourke is a kind of . . .

What?

I don't know how to say it but?

Jesus Christ, Con, I'm blue in the fucken face here.

There's a kind of witchery about him.

———

Next and upon the heels of trepidation Sheriff Devane approached the remains of the Zagreb Boarding House. The proprietor waited for him by the blackened mouth of its former entrance.

Mama Horvat, he said, tipping the brim of his hat with a nervous forefinger.

She looked at him as though at a damaged child. About her features was the pain of a great betrayal, and sadly she smiled—

Now I am the mama of these ashes, she said. Now I am the mama of fire and destroyment.

She sighed a great valley of sorrow, and surveyed it. Then—

Where is this Tom Rourke?

It's what we're shapin' to find out, Mama.

She smiled again at the hopelessness of that, and spoke quietly—

The boy Rourke was in the employment of the night, she said. He did not sleep so much as the churchyard bat. If two nights in seven he made it to his own bed it was the cause at her breakfast tables of remark and worry—was the mad little Irish motherfucker sick? If he was not about the bars and the dope of Celestials and the houses of the whoredom then he was inclined to walk the boards of the Zagreb the whole night through. Often he spoke out loud as he walked and spoke crazy. It was as though he was trying to make contact with such figures as might be found on the far side of the night. Maybe he wanted to be with them, she said. Perhaps even so young he wished to cross over.

Do you mean he wanted to die, Mama?

She laughed at that and raised to a point her ferocious chin—

They is calling out to him, she said.

Is a kind of singing, she said.

Is like choir of dark angel.

———

The silence of the new house grew oppressive. Its rooms were broad and rang with childless echoes. What was all of it for now? Anthony Harrington loosened with the tip of a knife the threaded ends of a horserope and rebraided them more tightly and tied them off to make the whip's point. He burnt the point over a candleflame to seal it. He removed his shirt and knelt on the floor and looked out the window and spoke to the East Ridge—

Jesus Christ Almighty, forgive me, he said.

A pale fury burned in the godhaunts of his jealous grey eyes. He wrapped the horserope thrice about his waist and cinched it and over the left shoulder he began to whip himself in a slow, rhythmic assault—

Mary, Mother of God, forgive me, he said.

The rope snapped out a slow, unceasing beat, and with each swing it took on venom, and the foul words that never crossed his lips in life flew madly about the cesspit of his mind—

oh you stupid fucken sufferin loolah to be taken in by a cunten rip the like of it the waft of the gutter off the guzz-eye whore and you were sold to the dream of it for the warmth of her clutch at night her grunt and girlish clasping and oh sweet Jesus Christ don't let me into a room with little cunt-faced Tom Rourke or what I won't do to the yappin bastard sweet Jesus Christ above on the cross I beseech thee don't let me give into the heart you callous thorn-bled motherfucker to leave me in a state the like of it to curse me with stupidity the like of it I who have done everything at your bidding and beck and oh God forgive me but I'll kill the little

bastard I'll cut his cock off and I'll shoot her in the fucken
gowl and straighten the eyes in her fucken head for her and
my men look on me now with sympathy oh poor aul Long
Ant'ny they say he'll not crawl back from this one lively oh
they laugh at me now in their filthy fucken bars and they've
already got songs about me probably and a sheriff that's a
drunk or else a fucken halfwit to be dealin with and oh just
let me into a locked room with that weaselmouthed Rourke
spawn and his runnin fucken lip and I'll take the tongue out
of his bastard head and that'll be him tongueless for good
and cunten glory hey

With that he collapsed onto the floor and sobbed. Thin
lines of blood ran tributaries the length of his back. It
could be said that Long Harrington hated especially the
eloquent. Words dropped from his own lips like stones.
He could put not warmth nor humour in them. It was
not that he did not feel such things. He had been lonely
in his life always but never before heartbroken. He saw
once more her crooked smile. The gentle swelling of
her hips. She could bear children he was certain. He
felt again her sly touch. He saw her darkened against
the morning light as he came up the hill from the night
shift. It was her slightness that beguiled. He would go
beyond the law if necessary for the vengeance required.

At the Lonegan Crane photographic studio, Sheriff Devane removed his hat and inclined his head to consider the proprietor. Jesus Christ alive—

The deathhouse pallor.

The gin-blossom eyes.

The darting asylum glances.

Also, the way there was something inescapably *feathery* about the little man—he is like a despicable bird, the sheriff decided.

Huddled in his wingback chair Lon Crane in turn considered the lawman with a weak but arrogant smile, as if he knew exactly what Devane was after.

I'm stood here and I'm fucken waitin, Lonnie?

But the silence held another slow moment between the men and was set in relief by the noise of the town at Monday's noon—

The paperboys' hollers and railroad screeches; the chaos of the pits; the tuneless percussion of the Quartz Street smiths; the humming of the bars and the eating houses in a rush-hour fluster; the roars from the cardgames, and from the sessions of bawd.

It could be heaven or it could be hell, the sheriff mused, as Lon Crane emerged from his huddle at last—

Don't pin it all on the boy, Dev.

Okay then . . .

Think about the young lady. Though I use the word under advisement.

Did he talk about her?

Well. He been at his ballad-makin, ain't he?

I see.

And more so's than usual.

A bad case of it then?

Not a love dose so much. In my opinion.

Oh?

Tom Rourke? It's all he's ever dreamed of is being the outlaw type. The lady, so-called? She might be a step ahead in that game.

What did he say about her?

That she come from trouble times.

Ah give me somethin to fucken feed on, Lon . . .

That's all he's said, Dev! Maybe it's back east you want to send your enquiries.

The photographer staggered to his cabinet. He had the look about him now of dying poultry. He took out the prints of the Harrington matrimonial and offered them. The sheriff raked an eye over the couple. There wasn't a woman alive who'd reckon she had a winning ticket stood there with the long God-botherer attached to her. He took in hand the bride's own portrait. She looked wistfully back at him over a thin shoulder, with a little mole or a dark blemish to its blade . . . Which was stirring, admittedly.

Pretty enough, I s'pose, the sheriff said.

In an off-the-street kind of way, Lon Crane said. You'll note the gleam of eye? Mischief in it. You'll note the urchin mouth? The little pout? I tell you now her word's not worth penny ha'penny.

He was in love with the fiend Rourke, and she had stolen him away—this could be read clearly, the sheriff felt.

How long's he worked for you, Lon?

In and out of here three years and some. Bright enough when he wants to be and if he's not in the dope too deep. Believes himself half a genius, actually. Which is a stretch by any reckon. He'll come to a bad end now though, won't he?

It wouldn't be lookin too good, the sheriff agreed.

Thomas Rourke speaks to the dead, Dev. Did you know this?

You'd hear it around the place, the sheriff said, thinking now of his desk, the low drawer, the Powers Special.

He's in consort with them, Mr. Devane. He believes that he'll be with them soon enough. He's not long for the stations is the boy's own read.

He could be right enough there.

And you know what that means?

Lon Crane smiled lavishly—

It means he might do anything now, Dev.

Who the fuck was he telling? The deathhauntedness of the Irish brethren was frequently a complication in the working life of Sheriff Stephen Devane. Soaked in an ambience of death from the cradle, they believed themselves generally to be on the way out, and sooner rather than later, and thus could be inclined to put aside the niceties of the living realm. Terrible people, born of a terrible nation.

Where would he run to, Lon?

Would be only an opinion I'd warrant.

Go on then?

That boy's face is set westwards for the sun. Always has been. He just want to sit back on his hindquarter with a dope pipe to hand and bloody apricate.

California then?

Not so he's said as much but.

With a shiver of intuition the sheriff saw now the lovers' flight. He saw its likely trace south by the mountains and through the Beaverhead. For Pocatello they were bound, and passage west? If you had to put a careful dollar on it. He picked up the portrait of the bride again and considered it more closely than was warranted.

Will she print okay for the posters?

'Nough to frighten the crows, Lon Crane said.

———

Now at that time in the city of Butte a boarding house of low repute named the Atlantic stood on the wrong end of Broadway amid the grinding hustle of that district and it was in a room there that a seven-foot-long (and half-as-broad) Cornish gunsman name of Jago Marrak searched for his boots through a whiskey-grained fug. Oh and it was a ripe condition Jago found himself in this bleak morning—

His noggin end was a tower of screeching bats, as of some haunted West Country moor; his stomach was a failing metropolis; his vision was blurred and flickering. He stumbled and groaned and bounced from the walls. He found his boots if only by the touch and wept his way into them. He staggered to the pisspot and aimed for it out of some remnant delicacy. He relieved himself fully to the roar of oceanic applause. He stood gormlessly then with drained apparatus to hand and tasted the sourness of his life—a melancholic, slave to the infinite sadness, he wondered if he might get through the day without opening his throat. Fuck it, he could try.

He went to the window and buttoned himself off and twitched an unspeakable net curtain hung with three summers' weight of petrified flycorpse and looked out grimly to the morning—

Winter in Butte.

Town of whores and chest infections.

Smell the pleurisy and the rotting lungs of it from a mile off.

It was a rum old bugger of a place to be laid up in. Also he was against the mountain air on a philosophic basis. It made a man light-headed and overly inclined towards company of an evening.

The night previous came back now in flits and terrible slivers, and let it be said that Jago Marrak was not yet beyond blushing. He had drank too deeply. He had lost a great deal of money at cards. He had come in a woman's shoe. Jesus Christ, Jago. There was a mother that loved you once. He staggered to the bed and sat on its edge. An appointment, wasn't there, for noon of this day? A conversation? His young countrymen might know of it. They slept yet in the adjoining room or else they'd died off sleeping—he would not put it past the dozy cunts. He pounded a fist on the wall to rouse the bastards—

Kitto!

Caden!

Not so much as a whimper nor a moan was returned and now Jago felt a weird presence at the back of his throat. Sweet death come closer, was it? He clutched at his throat and the feeling passed and he believed for a terrible moment that he might live. He sat on the edge of the bed and groaned voluptuously. From the floor he picked up some pages of his hopeless scribbling and storymaking and squinted at the pages for a moment and it was as much as he could do not to evacuate his bowels. Doomed romances, was it? He raised his head by evil inches and found his baccy and pipe and made an absolute fucking puppetshow of trying to fill the thing, the pipe shaking as if by the Devil possessed, the baccy falling to the floor. He cried again bitterly for his men—

Caden!

Kitto!

No response. The scuts was about their filthy dreams still. He looked up in beseechment at a section of cracked mirror on the wall. No man deserved the face that Jago Marrak had been cursed with at the age of forty-two. Face? It was a warscape, a scarred battlefield, an Agincourt—the giant Marrak was unloveable and unkillable. He rose onto his feet and bellowed like a ditch-stuck cow and forced a matchbook to a grip between his shaking fingers and lit a fucking match and sucked on the pipe and got the burn going at last and it just about cracked open his cranium but he sucked hard and harder again and took down the reviving tars and settled somewhat. He collapsed onto his calamitously outsized rear-end and the bedsprings whined for mercy. He cooed at the calming silvers of the smoke. Yes, there was something for noon of this day. The sly Devane was sending somebody? Wasn't that it? The gunsman's great ox-like heart throbbed and laboured. His brain rattled. His vision for a moment cleared. Footsteps beyond and was that his door was knocked on? Struck him now that it must be noon already—

Come enter! he cried.

At once a long priest type object was before him. Apparition of greyface. It offered a priestly paw—

Captain Anthony Harrington, it whispered. Anaconda company.

I'm sorry for your fucken troubles, Jago Marrak said.

Is it written on my face, friend?

Nobody come visit me that ain't got troubles, Cap.

Caden Spargo knelt and put a whiskey glass to the thin wall frame and cupped his ear to it and listened; Kitto Pengelly sat on the edge of the bunk and picked at his remaining teeth with a knife's tip and watched—

Fuck they sayin then?

Patient an' relax, boy.

Fuck you in the arse with a candle like yer hoor mother.

An' I'd be as grateful for it as she were. Now hush and let me listen, boy. I'm waitin on a price be named.

Hey but Caden?

Shut yer fucken cakehatch, Kit!

Yeah but who's died off and gone to heaven and made this ol' cunt the gaffer then? Ask thysel' that ever?

He took you from the gutter, did he not? Down Bristol dock? You was sellin your hole for an ham roll.

A libel afore noon. You're outdoin yoursel'.

Hush now . . . Okay then . . . There's two of 'em wants findin . . . A man and a woman.

I'm tirin of this ol' game.

What else you got on then?

I'm thinkin on a parcel of land, actually.

What you know from land?

Plenty, actually.

My hairy arse! What you gonna do? Set up an hog ranch?

Might do.

You'll be sat there? In the pale moonlight? Pullin at your snib-end and the hogs has got fever and is atein each other alive.

You got a nasty turn to your imaginin, Caden.

Aw hush and let me listen, Kit!

Okay then.

He's an Irish has gone south.

Filthy bastards. I hate an Hibernian. Always has done.

She's the man's wife.

A wife is it?

Kitto Pengelly, his interest at last aroused, came and knelt beside his countryman—

Dirty Irish, he said. Usually they's more interested in the drink. Gimme that glass, Caden . . .

Hush but?

Blood vengeance? Is what's asked for?

The Irish go ahead and do your worst, boys. Wifey-wifey brought back in the one piece.

Must be she's a looker hey?

We'll find out. There's photographs.

Oh aye?

Hush now. Note's being set.

———

The agreement was spat and shook on. The note was agreed at five thousand dollars. Jago Marrak would set out with his men in pursuit of the named parties. Further word had been taken from the town. It was surmised by now that they planned to make for San Francisco. They were keeping clear of the railroad yet. There was word of sightings throughout the Beaverhead country. Jago would follow with his men in that direction. The outlaw pair would have to pass through the junction then. There was no other way.

And so it was that three Cornish guns rode south for Pocatello—

Jago Marrak took point on a premium roan sourced out of the Ten Sleep in Wyoming. He wore a greatcoat of blonde furs against the November snow. Kitto Pengelly and Caden Spargo wore canvas and denim longcoats respectively, and were of somewhat lesser horse.

The men left the city of Butte that same evening at a glamorous canter.

There was an air of dark balladry about them as they went.

Their eyes were directed straight ahead and fixed to their sombre task.

From the sections and the street corners and from the swivelling turns of the bar stools the city watched them as they raced by and wondered who it was they were sent out for and pitied whoever the fuck it was.

———

Hey but Jago?

I don't want to hear it.

But the Beaverhead's an whole heap of country, no?

Stop with yer bloody bedwettin, the pair of ye. We can spread out the territory. There's fucken three of us, ain't there?

Silently (though with his lips moving) Jago Marrak tried to compose the words of it as he led his men into the winter mountains. He saw the lovers dispersed. He saw the guns in trail of them. He felt the great charge of brokenheartedness that was left in the story's wake.

He heard the sombre music of the mountain passes; he listened to the eeriness of the forest deep. He had more than his characters in mind—he had them in perfect likeness on photographic paper.

———

They rode for two nights and three days. They crossed paths with parties both known to them and unknown and further information was gathered by means that were sometimes coy and sometimes invasive.

By the end of the third day they felt certain they had closed ground on the runaways. They stopped to make a supper fire. They ate a stoneweight of alleged pork and drank coffee and smoked. Jago Marrak looked up to the stars in a glaze of creation and silently composed his long billowing sentences. Caden Spargo looked side-long to the giant man and wondered about his colouring. Kitto Pengelly studied with a vexed and sombre brow the portrait of the recent bride—

Pretty li'l maid, ain't she? An' waxin onto dirtylookin kinda? In the turn-eye?

Aw gimme that an' thy greasy paw!

I'm only fucken lookin, Caden.

He'll be havin one off the handle nex' thing, Jag!

Boy's monstrous.

Maid's got a pleasant little snout though, ain't she? I'd 'ave in the back door you gimme half a chance. Oh its southwards this young rake'd be headed.

Put down the fucken photograph, Kit!

Caden and Jago shared an educated glance—they had been witness to the Pengelly infatuations before, and knew where they could lead.

This right here is a professional fucken team, Jago Marrak said. An' we operates in a professional fucken manner.

Says you? An' your misdemeanours? An' not a lady's boot safe in the district?

Jago Marrak raised an open palm in warning towards Kitto then—

Enough, he said.

The teams that rode out in the territory had methods that were by this time greatly refined. They knew how to reduce the range quickly. The next day, acting on the word of a trusted confidant in the town of Lima, Jago Marrak decided on a south-eastering course towards the Centennial Mountains. He ordered his men to ride ahead to Pocatello to block the path westwards also. They would not depart his company without remark nor harangue—

Now I'm just speakin my mind here, gaffer?

An' I'm sure there's those'd like to hear it, Kit. I ain't among 'em.

Yeah but Jago?

Nor will I suffer your fucken witterins, Caden!

But say you find the run-offs while we's ahead in Pocatello? What's to stop you headin back for Butte and settlin the note?

It's a honest question, Jago . . .

Ye'd spake out agin my word and honour? To my fat bastard face? Oh it's a pair o' thankless cunts for countrymen I been cursed with! Away ye now to Pocatello!

Sourly his compadres rode off for the junction town, and Jago Marrak was glad to ride lonesome in the snow-clad silence for a while.

———

The lovers' creek ran on a quick decline. The clear water gasped and hissed over the black stones. The sound it made was youthful. The creek was not so broad you wouldn't think about jumping it. Nobody had ever put a name to it. It probably fed the Red Rock someplace. Nobody had ever followed its course to find out. It was hidden away in a stand of ancient timber. Spruce and whitebark pine and juniper dominated. The light among the trees was hazed and elegiacal. The sky was darkening to a greenish and glowering tone. The stars were already out. Antelope Peak stood distantly and in sombre judgement but it was fading quickly to the darkness. The creek was not far from the Monida Pass.

In the very last of that day's light Jago Marrak caught a dull shock of colour against the snow on the creek's bank. He dismounted from the roan. A woman's red wool sock lay on the bank. He picked it up and ran its fabric slowly between thumb and forefinger. He put the sock to his face and sniffed it. He stored it in an inside pocket of the furcoat. He tied off the roan. There was a waft of woodsmoke now. Just a scratch of it on the air. He walked in its direction. An empty green bottle poked from the snow. He picked it up and read the label. Saint Augustine wine. Pelee Island vineyard of Ontario. What did he remember of Augustine? Saint Augustine of Hippo was fascinated by those who could foretell the future but declared the diviners of horoscopes to be common swindlers. So the pedlars of this old piss as wine. He threw the bottle to the briars. He followed the woodsmoke. A solid huntsman's shack announced itself as Providence. A firelight burned in there. He approached quietly. He pushed in the door and looked down on the lovers and spoke gently, his lips soft with malice.

Streets of Pocatello

He spoke in the accent of the West Country—he was a Cousin Jack, a Cornish. The shotgun that hung by his side didn't need to be levelled to hold them fixed in place. They were frozen right where they lay. The Jack beast was of an indeterminate age and inclined his great slab of a head to the one side and considered the scene—

Rabbit-lookin boy's laid up with the urchin come west out of Chicago, he said. Is the report that needs makin. And thems interferin with each other in a prop'ry ain't theirs.

He dragged the door shut behind and stepped in closer and goddamn it if he didn't look bigger again. He shucked off a spectacular greatcoat of blonde furs. He took off his hat and beat the snow from it.

It's all the town's talkin 'bout back there, he said. Rabbitboy make off with mine captain's wife and an horse belongin to a respectable gentleman not to mention an amount of money owin to the Croat peoples I believe.

I always got on great with your crowd, Tom Rourke said. With the Cornish boys?

That's good to hear, the Jack said.

Polly Gillespie meantime thought there was nothing to lose in playing it light and she looked up to the gigantic type and said brightly—

Whyn't you haul down the moon while you're up there?

The Jack smiled kindly at that and snorted his nose in merriment and wiped it on the sleeve of his shirt. He set the shotgun by the wall. He sat down by the firepit and took out a pipe and lit it and smoked and looked about as relaxed as your grandaddy.

We could make an offering, Tom Rourke said. Cash money.

What I'd say for now, the Jack said, is why don't you shut yer rabbit mouth and roll back them blanket. I want to have a look-see.

We can be gone out of here in five minutes clean, Polly Gillespie said. Be like we never been.

But the Jack stood again and approached the pair where they lay and they flinched and he reached down and pulled back the blanket and closed his eyes and mumbled under his breath a moment as though in want of forgiveness from the strange god that must have reigned above his actions. Then—

Now let's see Rabbit do his business, he said. Have in and fuck her for me, boy.

The worry of it was he didn't look like he was making fun.

'Fore he get himsel' skinned up and racked, the Jack continued, I'll allow Rabbitboy one more shot for Nirvaner.

Ah now, Tom Rourke said.

The Jack wheezed then and loosened some lung phlegm and he sat down by the pit again and kicked the embers with his boot and stared into the embers as they briefly flared and he spat on the embers and considered the sizzle and then turned again to the lovers—

Jago Marrak is sat here waitin, he said. Now have in, Rabbit.

Ah look it, Mr. Marrak . . .

Hush boy and have in, he said. She got the turmuts for it certainly.

Easy now, big fella, Polly Gillespie said.

At this the Cornish name of Marrak rose once more and took up the furcoat and searched inside and took out a long hunting knife that had a scimitar tip to it and the look of unreasonable evil.

There's one or two scorch-lookin Croat peoples back there might not be incline to allow Rabbitboy any more joyful times 'fore he goes to meet his maker, he said. But they'll be happy enough I've had his lad off 'fore I fetch him back to justice, won't they? That'll be a certain end o' captains' wives for Rabbitboy.

Ah now, Tom Rourke said again.

Natural justice, Jago Marrak said. It's what a gunsman's sent out for. And if Rabbitboy don't bleed out in meantime he'll face the law as eunuch kind. There's more of 'em about than you'd reckon on actually.

He came still closer to the pair and towered above them—

Now go 'head and kiss her li'l baps for me, he said. Once more for the memories.

His voice came down to a huskier tone, and with every note that it dropped his colour rose by the same degree precisely—

Kiss 'em for me now, Rabbitboy, oh do . . .

The more quietly he spoke the more certainty there was that he needed to be obeyed. The pair fixed their clutches on each other or tried to and they began to kiss or tried to. Frightfully and in a warm fluster Jago Marrak was about his trouser buttons. He leant to pick up one of Polly Gillespie's boots then and suffered at the effort of it.

Now then Missus Mine Cap'n, he wheezed. Take his rabbity lad in hand and make her come up to size.

Sir there isn't a hope in fucken hell . . .

Shut yer rabbit mouth boy and let her have in!

The Jack stood above them and towered at his full length and took a slow and difficult breath. It caught badly with him. He began to make a thrumming sound that neither of them would forget. He rubbered his lips in a manner that was without grace. He tried to gather himself but it did not work. He looked boyish for a moment. Innocent somehow, and wanting. A rush of unnatural colour rose up swiftly from the region of his chest then. He did not appear surprised at this turn. He went to his knees and clutched at his throat and tipped over sideways. It was like a tree was felled, the way the Jack went down, first slowly, and then quick, and the stench of his last waste as a final insult putrefied the room—Jago Marrak was at once and formally quite dead. All the broad and ignorant seven foot of him.

A long and tricky silence ensued.

Then—

Lord Jesus reigns in the skies of heaven, Polly Gillespie said.

His mercy, Tom Rourke said. Pourin down on us by the fucken new time.

He got to his feet, tentatively, and circled the dead man. He grew relaxed about things—

Massive stroke, he said. I seen it before one time. At the Board of Trade. A coffin-maker out of Ballyvourney.

Ah but Jesus, Tom?

When your luck runs, Polly? It most surely does run.

———

From the dead Cornish gigantic type they took the greatcoat of blonde furs and a fresh shake of more than sixty bucks—they were putting together a bankroll, there was no doubt about it. They took also the shotgun and the evil knife and were sombre proud at the feeling of being weaponed up finally.

There was a sense of purpose about them now. They were awake to the world again. They came upon the roan. They concluded quickly that they had not the handling of it. After an amount of trial and error Tom

Rourke managed to free the saddle from the roan and was proud not to make a complete buzzard of the job. He untied the horse and set it free with a slap to the rump and they watched the horse disappear into the winter forest.

Together, and by no means in a smooth operation, they managed to switch up the gunsman's hand-tooled and most capacious saddle for the palomino's worn and shabbier effort. The palomino didn't know herself in such finery—she pranced daintily as if wanting a picture made and even showed a gummy smile. The horse was getting to be too fucking much in places, was Polly Gillespie's opinion, but she held on to it, knowing how sweet he was on the old tart.

They rode out at last and Tom Rourke could not even look back at Providence as they left it behind.

Oh fuck, Polly, he said.

I know, she said. I know it, sweetcake.

And at once it was gone and it faded into their twined past and they made aim for the Pontneuf river that would take them to the Utah & Northern at Pocatello Junction and the passage west and their new lives under the California sun.

They rode for careful hours through the cold fabrics of darkness. There was a trail on them now for sure. They made no fire when finally they did stop. They lay wrapped in amalgamated wintercoats against the base of a noble tree. They didn't feel the cold for the thrill of new fear that was laid atop it. The next morning they rode on with purpose and still with the fear.

Better if I take the gun, she said. Stow it on my lap this way.

Don't know if it looks right.

It's better if I have it.

It's uncouth is what it is.

Who's lookin at us, pilgrim?

Okay then.

You can take the knife.

Crumbs from the table.

You look awkward with the gun, Tom. Is all I'm sayin here. Many times you shot one off?

Not sayin I have done ever.

You're elbows and thumbs with it.

It's not the point of the matter.

I've shot one off a bunch of times.

When was this?

Take the knife, she said. Just stow it careful and don't cut yourself.

Kind of a fucken halfwit you take me for?

I think your mind travels some.

I deny it. And when'd you shoot a gun off exactly?

Old Jed back at Saint Dom's . . .

Oh I've heard all about the man.

. . . he used take me on turkey shoots.

Old Jed gave you instruction?

Yessir.

What else was he offerin?

S'up with you, Tom Rourke?

Many turkeys you shoot?

I definitely winged a share of them bitches.

Was this Jed character interferin with you, Polly?

So what? So now you're jealous-minded on an old Scotch that's dead and gone the best part of twenty years?

It's the way my head turns. I'm sorry about it. It's a sickness that I have.

Okay.

I mean try livin this bullshit from the inside out, Poll.

The forest was a machine that made ice. The lungs rasped on every drawn breath. At evening deep in a clutch of fir they risked a small fire against the freezing air and they sat with it. The stars were the same old stars, the trees the same. She saw the doubt in him even as he spoke out against it—

Pocatello's a wide-open town, he said. There'll be all sorts passin through. We'll be lost in the crowd is what I'm tellin you.

I got a bad feelin though.

We have to go through Pocatello. We have to get on the rail, Polly. There's no other way.

I know it.

We're headed for the sea is what it is.

Ain't stoppin 'til I smell the salt.

We got an agreement. Stamped. It's not natural to live away from the sea.

And there's me that never lived by it not yet.

I wasn't right in myself in Butte. On account of the no sea. Day one I wasn't right.

Yeah but listen.

What?

You understand we're leavin this horse behind?

I know it.

And how'd you feel about that?

Not great, Poll.

They lay beneath the Marrak furs but did not sleep. The night was clear and bitter cold with the stars in bright clusters above the firtops. They could make out the constellations everybody knew. The Plough, and the Dog Star, and so forth. They foostered a little with each other but neither was agitated enough for taking a layer off. They flopped and turned. Then—

Hey look it, she said.

What?

'Nother pocket.

She took a couple of items from a pocket hidden deep in the Jack's furcoat. He leaned in beside, and they examined the items—

First was a wrinkled photograph showed a woman about sixty years old and hardy-handsome, with the air of country stock, and there was the certain look of a mother about her, too, and they were both quiet about that for a moment, wondering if she was alive still, wondering if she could sense that her prodigious boy was no longer so, wondering if she was inclined to gaze up at the sky herself and go dreaming, wondered if tonight she'd see the same old stars, and they got to thinking sombrely on that, and got to knowing there was a lot of sadness in the world no matter what way you looked at it.

Second was a cutting from a Philadelphia newspaper of recent times that offered an article of instruction— The Twelve Rules for Writing Western Adventures. Tom Rourke took the cutting and studied it a while in grave and scholastic silence. Then, sourly—

There's fucken twelve of 'em?

Polly Gillespie in the meantime was rooting around in the furcoat again and now she came out with her own red wool sock and showed it—

The fuck? she said.

———

When a measure of sleep at last came that night it was in rags and snatches only and it was wretched. Sometimes in the dark he spoke as though in a delirium. She tried to make out the words of it. It was as if he was trying to cast a spell. Mutterings and soft moans were sent up to the treetops, to the cold moon. The fact was he could hear the voices of his significant dead. They were close to him now. There was a tremendous pull on him. She tried to hold him back from that pull. These transactions took place without words. They were worked out by the touch alone. They lasted until the first attempt at what a morning might look like started to show itself through the trees. They woke together. They lay there stiff and frozen and held hands.

Tom? I got a dose of the morbs.

We could start up a club, he said.

———

They had kept a track of the days roughly. You could always tell the Sundays. It must have been into December by now. The country was in the deep pit of the year. Through the winterbared trees a pair of runaways could no longer pass so easily.

They'll see us comin for miles out, he said.

Be like the circus is comin in, she said.

If Jago Marrak had tracked them, others could too. Maybe the Reverend had passed on word, or maybe the Métis. You could trust nobody in this country or not for long. The fear increased by increments with each passing mile that morning. The horse began to labour. They saw this and felt it but they made no comment on it. He got off and walked the horse for a while. The light was no more than a mean and taunting reminder of what light could be, a rumour of what light there once was. They talked against their fear. They talked of their lost times. She told him of the skivvying jobs she had worked and the friends and the enemies she had made, the latter being the less numerous but the easier somehow to recall. She was blurry about the details of things, he felt, but he did not press. He told of his old Butte adventures and all his forlorn and misdirected passions. He said little of the time before he came to Butte or where he had come from. He said the black dogs of the home place roamed the yards of his sleep and so he tried not to sleep and she sensed also not to press.

⬩

About noon one day they came on a broader course of river that could only be the Pontneuf. Followed by its course it would take them to Pocatello. They left behind the forest that had sheltered them. It was a pure lit winter on the riverbank. The water as it moved dragged a sparkling glister to traffic in the light above it. Now there were bodies about the world again. They passed a sitting of Nez Percé at a fire. She waved but there was no response, not a flicker beyond the flames. There were traders working a smoker on the far bank of the river and she waved at them and the men waved back and barked like comic dogs and rubbed their bellies. At intervals there were cattlemen heading south and home in small packs and in pairs and riding lonesome. The high country fell away to a great valley and in many places the snow had not yet settled and the horse fed more easily.

In San Francisco we'll talk about this.
 Be like a story that gets told.
 This'll be in a house on the bay.
 I can smell the air of it right now, Poll.
 And tell you what? That house will have a piano.
 All this will be in the long ago.
 Be like out of a dream.

———

In the distance the lamps of Pocatello burned through a veil of midwinter rain. A quartermoon made first appearance above the Pontneuf river. They stopped to brace themselves for the town. They climbed from the horse. They thought about things. They may have erred on the side of reason for a moment. Then they smiled it off and thought fuck it.
 I think we're ready, he said.

We ain't got nothin left to lose, she said.

It could not be said they weren't at some level enjoying the dark romance of the debacle. They might admit also to feeling a little more schooled about themselves after a time under the stars in the outlaw style. He swung up onto the horse again and offered his hand and she swung up behind.

Ride it like you own it, she said.

The junction town was announced by a scatter of poor domiciles that looked as if a raised voice might knock them flat. The lovers were watched carefully as they went by. He held himself with the shoulders squared and looked straight ahead and spoke to himself silently as he rode—

Bear down on the fucken world, he said.

That's right, she said, and said it aloud.

He wore a full beard by now and already there was some grey coming through in its wires and he looked closer to his years. She swung out a cool sideways glance this way and hither. The buildings they passed became more settled in their demeanour and established themselves by bricks and boards into the streets of a new town. There was a train moving in the far-off rainhaze and it was bluesy. The grey emerging in his beard so early was his nerves coming through, she reckoned, but kept quiet about that.

———

A migrant family stood engraved with its own misery on the edge of the main street. It looked as if the famine was on them. There was a mother and father and a clutch of children too weak to make fun or trouble even. It brought a shudder to see them. Like a sour turn from the Bible times the family was an assembly of jutting bones and sunken cheek-hollows and huge pleading eyes. He stopped up the horse. They climbed down and nodded how-are-yas. Polly Gillespie offered tins of saltfish and beans that were left over and the father accepted them and in thanks mumbled a few words of a Slav tongue. Tom Rourke passed over some dollars too and the burden of their guilt eased although briefly.

The rain fell on Pocatello. The Pontneuf river ran swiftly. The main street parted for them as they rode through. The candles of Noël burned in the windows already, their soft light doubled in the darkening glass.

It might have been remarked that the young couple held themselves with a particular arrogance as they went by and sported fanciful rag-scarves worn at the neck and about the wrists and it was on a very fine palomino they rode.

—

They dismounted outside the Perpetual Hotel. They took down the pack. A pale white-haired boy maybe with a touch of albino or Swede to him stepped out from the hotel and took the measure of them. He was about fourteen years old and solemn with the trials of it. He considered his boots at some length and nodded slowly as though he was coming to terms with the situation.

Hidee, he said.

Hello.

The boy raised and opened a palm to the sky and considered the rain.

Well, it ain't much, he said.

We been through worse.

I reckon so.

Town busy?

Busier than hell, he said, and that's a busy one.

Indeed.

Fixin to stay up a while?

If there's a room?

Oh there's rooms.

The boy was offered the rein but the horse recoiled at his touch on it, her every muscle tensing, her skin livid under the burn of the hotel lights.

Reckon she's a picky one, the boy said.

She's that.

An amount of connivance at length persuaded the horse to go with the boy to livery. As she was led away, she looked back to the lovers darkly, betrayed.

Everyday business was strange to transact having been so long removed from the swim of affairs. But they felt they'd arranged their faces as reasonably as they could for it and kept their voices steady.

The town was all life about them. The noise of the place was an astonishment. There was a louche music close by. It moved on a slow piano line and you could not but imagine louche dancing rolling out on the tow of it. There were the sounds of glasses and kitchens and taprooms foaming with all the good feeling of the evening.

There was a fat bankroll in the pocket that was surely burning a hole but they'd have to be careful how they spent it.

We get the room and keep to ourselves, she said.

Is what we absolutely fucken do, he said.

They entered the hotel. It was not a fancy place by any means but it felt like one after a time in the briars. Playing up an air of jauntiness he slapped the lobby wall with an open hand as they passed through and even whistled a bit. She was conscious of the waft they carried. They smelt like thirty days of country was the truth of it. Of course they'd never taken a room together before and she was proud of him when he walked right up to that desk and bamped the bell like he was born to it. He named them as marrieds and there was no one looking to see no ring.

They lay in the tub together in room number nine at the Perpetual Hotel. That soak was the greatest feeling that was ever had. She lay back with her head on his chest. She turned and with her finger traced out the fading scar of the P. They were so tired as to be beyond interfering with each other. All he had in him was to tap

out the line of a new air on her shoulder with his fingertips and he hummed it to her—it was a pretty one—and
they fell asleep right there in the tub water.

When they woke the water had grown cold and grey
around them and the night outside by a good measure the more raucous. No point in saying they weren't
tempted by it. They looked out and there were roisterers
at large all about the muddy streets and they traded a
glance—it really was a wide-open town.

We stick to the hotel, she said.

Absolutely, he said.

Even if it wasn't the fanciest establishment you could
have your food brought up and it took them a while to
decide on the makings of the feast. They settled on beef-
steaks and fried eggs and jacket potatoes with saltbut-
ter and they'd an insufferable wait for it. Their mouths
watered all the while they waited. It was brought up at
last by the same ghostly-looking boy and he brought the
bottles of red wine they'd ordered also. He set it all down
on the small table they'd dragged over to the window.

It's a feed, the boy said.

It surely is.

Hope it does ye a wealth of good.

Cain't do a body no harm, Tom Rourke said, and she wondered about this latest accent he was trying on.

As the boy departed he threw a hungry eye to the bed to see if it was ruffled already. They noted that and smiled proudly at it. They sat together and she poured the wine and they toasted each other shyly and without words.

They looked out as they ate. Travellers moved by cloaked against the night and rain. It was a woozy scene in the rain, the colours all blurred and ran. Each fork-load was worked on slowly and with great relish. There was quite naturally a feeling hanging above the meal that it could be their last one but neither of them made mention of it. That feeling was in the room with them though. He took her hand at one point and stared at her all soft-eyed and earnest as if he was edging up to a speech of the heart—

Keep it to yourself for once, she said.

They sat and drank the wine and smoked. They turned the lights off the better to savour the night-town glow of the streets outside. But they could not settle at all. They were too close to the territory of their offences yet. They knew now that they'd settle only when they felt the

California sun on their faces. He stood and went to the window and peered edgeways along the thoroughfare. There was nothing out there that had the look of closing for the night.

I could find out about tickets right now, he said.

Maybe we can get us out of here tomorrow?

Is what we should try.

He told her not to leave the room and to answer only to his knock—the knock was three times, a beat, and twice then. She did not look after him as he left.

———

She had not been alone for more than a month. The run of her thoughts was different when she was left to herself. She was not fond of the way they ran. She drank wine. She smoked. The whole plain world slipped into view again. Through the rain the lamps of Pocatello dulled and their light dissolved. She drifted through the streets of her old towns again. She closed her eyes and moved through the hatchwork of the forest light again. She worried about the horse a bit. She stood and went to the window and looked out. There were two men across the street from the hotel. They were staring right up at the room and they weren't making no pretence otherwise. They were just standing there beneath their hatbrims to keep the rain off and they hunched in the shadows casual as a pair of cornerboys and they smoked and looked up.

———

Tom Rourke walked the streets of the new town. The rain needled his face with hard pointed questions. It would be accurate to remark that he was not entirely gathered in himself. He believed again in the territories of heaven and hell. He believed in the territories of purgatory and limbo. He was not sure in which territory now he roamed. The river ran high and quick. He spoke in dark mutters against the rain and against the seeping nausea of doubt. He said over and again her name as he walked by the river. Her effect on him was measured easily by the weight of absence when he walked alone. He crossed the railroad yards in a black dream without her. A locomotive of the Utah & Northern roused itself like a great waking beast. It juddered along its sides and groaned and spilt its grease and hissed and smoked. Soon it would strike out west and cut the dark in two.

Maybe they could leave tonight—maybe this right here was the engine of their escape?

He found the ticket office at the moment precisely its shutters were drawn down by a jaunty little motherfucker with a poodle's crimped hair and shirt garters and bright avid eyes. He made protest but to no avail.

There is always a tomorrow, the man said, grinning.

He walked back through the town. By the river he was watched and remarked on. He could sense this without turning. He felt his breath shorten and break up and now it came in panicked stabs. He knew with certainty that the world had caught up and their luck was turning. He fled the streets in nausea and in fear and raced back to the hotel. The pale albino type boy was sat on the stairway with his head in his hands. The boy's aspect was of misery and remorse. The boy looked up and shook his head slowly. The door of room nine hung open. Two gunsmen sat on the bed and she lay on the floor in a mess of blood and pain already.

Oh Tom I'm beat pretty bad, she said.

S I X

Nightmusic

About this time it became the common perception that trains sounded lonesome, especially in the hours of darkness, and you could not deny it looking across the yards at Pocatello Junction on that rainy December night as the Utah & Northern went out for Salt Lake City and left a long forlorn calling in its wake. The rain came slantwise and harder now across the sheds and the yards and the depot. A pair of Chinese took bowls of green tea as they sat on their haunches in the doorway of their quarters. They looked out to the heaving rain and told again an old wry joke—what a paradise it was that awaited us at the far ends of the earth. There were lights in the carpenters' shop yet and the work of irregular sawings and grindings from there. The Slav family in quiet distress made a poor camp among the sidings and waited on their father's return. There was the distant roll of a piano line as it played in counterpoint to the night train's fading call. There was some distant jeering also. The quartermoon climbed by slow degrees through the cloudbank to add to the night's yearnful air and still the beating of the rain came down on the cars of the resting stock and somewhere in the town the jags of a woman's screeching were cut short.

———

The father of the Slav family made his way through the town at a little past midnight. You could cast the yearning also with his sombre image—a bony Herzogovinian farmboy huddled against the Idaho rain. He heard the woman's screeches but they were not his business. He had been promised what bread was left over once service was done at Kiesel's Eating House. He waited as instructed in the alleyway behind. He stood close in to the building against the rain. He was aware of the disturbance on the air. He could feel the bad thrill of it like a quickness in the blood. Down the way stood the back of the hotel. A farm wagon waited by its kitchen entry. Its horses were stoical and quiet in the rain. He wondered what deliveries were being made at this hour. He heard the trouble flare again. He knew it was from the hotel and then the screaming came up and it came closer and the sound of bootsteps and he huddled in tighter to the building and shut his eyes so as not to see.

———

The player stood up in a bad hissy and slammed the piano lid shut and the drunk stumbled in leering and raised the lid again. Play, he said. Fuck you, the piano player said. Leering all the wider the drunk found a filthy dollar bill and balled it up and stuffed it down the front of the player's shirt. I takes you home again, Kathleen, he said, you play that fucking tune right now. I play it on your motherfucker ass, the player said, how that be? The drunk leapt onto him joyously and they fell to the floor rolling and biting at each other and the great jeers that came up from the pasted imbibers still left on the premises were plenty enough to drown out the sounds of fracas in the alleyway beyond.

———

A travelling journalist in sufferance to his Scots origin hunkered down in his room at the Perpetual Hotel and stewed a pot of tea until it was about strong enough to take his own weight across the surface. He balled up his cotton plugs and stuffed them in his ears. He looked out to the rain and the last revels of the night and he was grateful for the muffled silence. He considered with sweet sorrow then the blank page of his journal, cursed once more his vocation, and settled to some note-making—

Pocatello Junction, he wrote, *is a wide-open town, the gateway to the northern and western regions, and to the last frontiers of our time.*

Just outside his window, yet beyond his witness, a farm wagon made chaotic pace along the town's main drag, its horses working in fast tandem and a pair of amplified men up back roaring them on.

Across the midnight yards, the Scotsman continued, *the Utah & Northern sounds lonesome as a prairie coyote in its eerie call . . .*

Now the farm wagon almost went up on the one wheel it made so sharp a turn towards the Pontneuf river.

. . . and the inscrutable Chinese of the sidings, known to all as the Celestials, stare into the rain as if to read messages in its dismal fall.

Before it disappeared into the murk of the night there were signs of struggle to be made out beneath the can-

vas draw pulled over the wagon's flatbed, and the Scotsman was pleased with the rhyme that had slipped into
his sentence, having not planned it at all, though he did
wonder who it was that first decided coyotes sounded
lonesome.

Few in this world has as much languor to spare as the
vagrant gentleman who took a bottle of sherry beneath
a rock outcrop on the bank of the Pontneuf that night.
Mother, dispense to me, he whispered, and the bottle
obliged. The sherry brought to his mind the swaying of
long dresses and the church gardens of old England. The
rain died off at last and left a freshness on the washed
air. The quartermoon came and went from beyond the
cloudbank as if it could not decide. From out of nowhere
a wagon appeared at pace with two men atop it and
aimed for the bridge. The gentleman took a nip from
the bottle. He was unsettled by the vision. His languor
now was broken. Where in the hell was a farm wagon
headed for at this hour and in a hurry? There was no
sense to it. He stood up with concern and he looked
after the wagon as it crossed the river—

I hope all this turns out okay, he said.

But quickly the air settled again and the quiet of a long December night came down on Pocatello Junction—

It was set in a valley. There was a wall of mountains to the north and east. The valley in the night was a great silent stage. The story could turn in any direction yet. If there was danger and cruelty around here in good supply, there was a surplus of possibility, too, and of hope. Anything could happen if you just aimed yourself in the right direction and you could get to a whole lot of places pretty fast from here—

You could rattle into Spokane or see the lights of Cheyenne or have a go up in Deadwood. All paths were open still. You could take your slice. Those who had been dispossessed would forever remain so—this was the golden promise of the Republic.

The Slav family was fed at last and slept, and for a brief while in their quarters the Chinese slept. The Scotsman slept and dreamed in clipped efficient paragraphs. The player paced the empty saloon a while and sat at his piano stool and raised the lid. He played a couple of blue notes over and again but they were not equal to the heartache that sustained the moment and the town. The gentleman of the riverbank slept and was blessed to not dream at all. The Pontneuf river carried its lost voices and was memorious. In room number nine at the Perpetual Hotel the window was left open to clear the air. The remains of the lovers' feast was laid out on the table by the window. There was half a bottle of red wine still to be drank. The albino-looking boy was on his knees on the floor and with a basin of hot water and suds and rags he worked to clean away the bloodstains.

SEVEN

In the House of a Deathlorn Swede

Tom Rourke believed that he had reached the Hereafter. Its light was a pale grey and of special radiance. The land was open and without feature but for the faint line of the horizon where the sky met an expanse of white plain. He was above the plain at a serene elevation. There was something beyond death after all. It was a kind of peace certainly. He was at a good distance from his old self. He was here but he was not here. The line of the horizon was a soft wound against the low belly of the sky. He fingered the wound gently and little pinprick dazzlebursts of sexual pleasure or in fact almost of pain were felt inside. He had pined for death for so long and had known always there was nothing about it to fear and here it was and as wonderful as he'd hoped for.

Now he just had to wait it out and she would join him here.

A creaking sounded to his easterly side. He tried to turn his head in the direction of it but he could not move at all. A steward of the Hereafter appeared before him wearing a black wool beret and a long grey shift. He was a male figure of about sixty years old if you were going by the terms of the mortal realm. He had arranged on a brass tray a mighty syringe. He wore a melancholy expression and did not speak nor gesture. He leaned in and searched for a vein and tapped one out and scratched it with the needle's tip and it clarified for Rourke that if the pure and eternal state of death was not yet his to savour then he had found instead the sweetest dope that ever was.

——

When he came to again a light snow was falling. The country was familiar but not. It was much as a place encountered in a dream. He had not entirely come loose from himself. He began to wake from the dream. He became unsettled. He closed his eyes and saw the room at the Perpetual Hotel again. The two men sat on the bed. They rose and came towards him. He opened his eyes sharply to the falling snow, the line of the horizon. He located the pain now in two places. His jaw was in sections and his gut was reefed.

She was not dead because he could hear her still. He closed his eyes and chased down the night at the Perpetual Hotel. She lay there bloodied and beaten with her mouth twisted into a terrible cry. The men spoke to him calmly. They were Cornish again and of a pack it seemed. Where's Jago? one said. The room was lit only by the lamps of the town beyond it. There were cries from the Pontneuf river and laughter. The men rose and came towards him. He opened his eyes to a creaking from the easterly side—

A solemn pale boy stepped into view and was a familiar ghost. The boy carried a steaming tin bowl and a cloth and he rinsed out the cloth in the bowl and applied it to Tom Rourke's forehead. He tried to speak to the boy but he could not make the words form. The boy continued at his nursing and spoke quietly—

Prob'ly you're gonna be okay, he said.

The pain became more pronounced. His gut sang out an evil whine. His leftside jaw moved on a trick hinge. He closed his eyes for the Perpetual Hotel—

He saw the flash of the knife and felt again the soft awe of its incision and felt again on his jaw the hard snap of the rifle butt swung and then her screams cut dead and the quickfallen blackness.

He opened his eyes. He shaped his lips but he could not speak. He knew that his words would come soon enough and that he would detest them. He longed to see the grim old man who was the needle's steward if not heaven's.

He could move his head from side to side now. He lay in a small bare room. The walls were of a clean white render. The cleanliness made him emotional. On the plain beyond the day was fading out to a bloodied winter dusk. There was an overwhelming air of Protestants.

He could trace the low slit across his belly and the stitches—he counted off a dozen at least. He talked to her for a while. He told her that it would be okay. He believed that she could hear him still.

It had fallen night when the old man and the solemn boy returned together. He could see now they were family to each other. The old man carried again the brass tray and the syringe and Tom Rourke knew that he was held in formal care. The boy came again with the tin bowl and the cloth. The man leaned in and searched for a vein and tapped one out and spoke—

Varför här den här mannen en sådan tolerans för morfin?

What he wants to know, the boy said, is how come you got such a taste for it?

Tom Rourke locked eyes with the old man in apology and if he could have spoken at all he would have confided freely that he had made some bad decisions in his life.

The old man anyway inserted the spike and hit the plunger and as the heat spread out he could tell at once there was less of it and that he was on a slow tapering now.

Han suger upp det som en svamp, the old man said.

The boy leaned in and mopped his brow—

Says you take it up like a sponge.

The old man pulled back the blanket and examined the belly wound. Rourke could not himself look down and was glad of that.

Drifts of rain moved across the sky and plain and he knew that he would live. The aching of his gut faded to a dullness. He worked at his jaw and tried to smooth out its movement. He looked out to the rain. He had not known her two months before—could he forget her again as quick?

He was at a point of remove from himself yet but he was waking in the body. He had the veins of his arms and he had the beating of his heart. The boy entered the room and it was only now by the solemn mooching of the gait that he recognised him as the albino type from the Perpetual Hotel and Tom Rourke was by another degree back in the world. The boy brought him a thin potato soup and a weak tea. He was spooned a taste of the one and fed a few sups of the other. His words came at last if weakly—

How long?

The boy looked out sombrely, as though the reckoning of it was written on the sky or plain.

I guess that was the Friday, he said. Now we got us the Wednesday.

The boy told it to him after a sorrowful and halting style. He had known at once, he said, that there was no way of bringing the law into it. They had taken the woman and they were not to be stopped in this life. Yes they were Jacks but they didn't seem to like each other too much. The woman was bloodied but she could walk the last that he saw of it.

I got your pack here, the boy said. The rifle went with 'em.

The horse?

It's looked after.

He made himself stronger by force of belief. He spoke to God fiercely. On the evening of the day following he was helped from the bed by the boy and he walked the short length of the room and back and then he drank water and tea and spooned down some more of the potato soup and ate a rye bread. He slept like the dead after that. There was no more dreaming. When he came to again the old man was before him in the morning light. He pointed to himself—

Bergman, he said.

Tom Rourke nodded in sombre acknowledgement and they spent a few silent moments together and conferred without speaking and it was companionable.

The boy came in with a couple of soft-boiled eggs and some more of the rye bread and coffee.

Old man Bergman watched him as he ate and seemed satisfied with the course of the recovery. Then he looked away discreetly to the white fields of the winter sky. He murmured to the boy sidelong and in the tongue of the Swedes again—

Vad har den här mannen gjort?

He wants to know what it is you done, the boy said.

Very slowly and painfully Tom Rourke spoke the truth or at least the truth as he saw it. He said that in his actions he had been guided not by lustfulness nor by greed. He had been steered by fate, he said. He believed he was acting as though under the pull of the moon and tides. He had about as little say in it as that. He needed to be with this person and now that she had been taken from him he needed to follow and find her. If death came in the way of seeing her again in this life, that was just how it was meant to be, and he was not afraid. For the first time in his life, he said, he was not afraid.

The old man took all this in and weighed it. He spoke at length then, with the boy following in careful translation—

Du föddes under en mörk stjärna.

What he reckon is you was born to a dark star.

Gospel, Tom Rourke said.

När du föds på ett sådant sätt betyder det att det inte finns något hopp om ett tillfredsställt liv.

Says for folks born that way, you can about throw your hat at it. There ain't much hope of satisfaction, not in this life.

Amen, Tom Rourke said.

The old man gestured to the plain and the open sky then, and he was dismissive of it all—

Detta löjliga land kommer att berätta sagor för dig.

In a country like this, the boy said, all they give you is fairy tales.

De kommer att berätta är att lycka är möjlig och i själva verket är det ditt öde.

In this country? the boy said. They'll tell you that you can be happy. That it's your right and destiny.

Det här är hästskit.

Now that's a bunch of horseshit.

Lycka är inte det vanliga mänskliga uppnåendet.

Happiness ain't generally how it works out for folks.

Kom ihåg att vi bara fördriver tid till vår ound-vikliga död.

Remember always that we're only markin time until sweet death comes, and it's surely comin for us all.

God be good to us, Tom Rourke said.

Om det finns någon där ute som kan hjälpa dig att lindra smärtan i din existens . . .

So if there's someone out there who can help you to ease the pain of your life . . .

. . . så ska du göra vad du än behöver göra för att vara med henne.

. . . then he reckon you gotta go an' do what it is you gotta do.

EIGHT

Polly Got the Morbs

Looking back on it now it can feel like a different person entirely was carried out from the streets of Pocatello that night. It felt like she was being carried out of one life and into another when she heard the water moving and the wagon crossed the Pontneuf river as though across the Styx of sombre legend and into the unknowable dark that waits on all souls or so they'd tell you. The wind had died off and the rain had stopped and she could hear the bawling of the bitch foxes in heat and the eerieness of the coyotes and the mad skittering of her own heart and the horseteam working and the evil scraping of the wheels over and over again as she lay there gagged and tied and hid up under a canvas draw in the cold black night.

The Jacks were at their snapping and grousing up

there. She could make out by the tone of it they were bartering with each other. There wasn't anything settled about none of it was her read. She could make out some of the words too and a thing she remembered ever after was when one of them said hey now give that horse his head, meaning to whup one of the horses and go quicker, but what she saw then was like a picture appearing out of the darkness and just floating there, was a headless horse like out of a bad dream, like out in the deep haunt-edness somewhere, like out in the strange far country we all roam in our sleep.

A rip in the canvas showed a strip of black clouded sky and they moved on and the wheels creaked and turned and sparks flew up to the black of the sky and disappeared and she prepared herself for whatever was coming next or she tried to.

She'd been kicked and beaten in the hotel room. She'd been thrun down and spat on and called every name from harlot to whore and back again and others she hadn't even heard of yet. One of them came at her harder than the other was what it felt like. Tom Rourke got back then and took the worse share of it again and he was down and reefed and battered on the floor bleeding out and his eyes were closed or closing the last she saw of him.

Maybe the pale horse-stabling boy was in on it she reckoned maybe that albino-looking Swede type motherfucker had been bought off.

She tried to fight back in the room throwin out her fists and again when they got her outside but it turned out that a woman kicked around an alleyway like a piece of meat and all beat up at midnight with a filthy hand locked to her jaw didn't raise an eyebrow not in Pocatello—so this is what they mean by a wide-open town hey?

Now it felt like they were climbing. She took to making a low humming noise beneath the gag for comfort. It was like a drone sound made with the lips against the rags that near enough choked her and she kept it going against the pain and the evil. If she could think just about making that slow and longdrawn sound and working on it she wouldn't have to think about nothing else that was happening. Surviving was what it was called and she was schooled in it.

The wagon stopped and the men climbed down. She heard them walk off a distance and the needling sound of their dispute came up and now those Cornish fucks they was really going at it.

She lay under the canvas draw. Crazy words came through her mind and ran amok. The word *chattel* came through her mind and ran. It was like another sour turn from the Bible times.

What we got us here, she thought, is one of those rank evil type nightmare situations, and it wasn't like she hadn't been through a share of them before.

One of the Jacks barked hard at the other then and she thought she heard a fist slapped. Wet sound of it. Bone on skin. And the silence again.

Silence held a while.

She lay in the darkness and sermonised against herself. If you are of the kind that throws yourself to the fates of the earth then you better watch out. If you are of the kind that takes notions in a life then you just got to accept all of that life's capricious outcomes. If you are of the kind that throws all cares to the wind don't go complainin when suddenly you are off your goddamn feet and spinnin out forever in the crazy fucking wind. Now I have no longer the agency of my own affairs, Jesus, and that is a goddamn fact.

Was she carried as chattel now?

She tried to pray but nothing came of it. There was no God not on this mountain road. She closed her eyes and saw the Perpetual Hotel again and Tom Rourke lay there bleeding out from the gut. The way his mouth was set he looked like a small boy about to die off. She opened her eyes and looked up through the rip in the canvas and into the black sky and somehow (again) it was as though she was above it all and looking down and now the clouds moved real slow and the moon showed itself for half a minute and there was fires on the moon and she knew that he was breathing.

She knew also he was not cut out for this kind of life. He might have had some chance if they never would have met at all. I have led another one astray, oh Jesus, won't you please help him out now?

The Jack voices came up again. One of them was on the wheedling and cajoling side of it but the other was not to be pacified and was in the vicinity of losing the grip entirely. The argument continued and faded off into the night again and she reckoned they were taking the talk out of earshot from her and that was in no way a comforting thing.

The foxes and the coyotes in the meantime those howling bitches were in a contest to see who could make the night sound more full of crazy sex and the bone evils and they was both winning and Polly Gillespie lay in the dark with her bright blue eyes staring wide open into the night through the canvas rip and she made the slow droning noise against the gag and kept it going like a motherfucker and kept it going some more.

She tried to breathe steady and even.

She tried to gather herself in.

She had known evil before after all—

She knew the strange thing was it made everything slow down when it happened. The world went into a kind of swooning and everything woozed out. The walls went soft and melted down and the floor sank away beneath your feet and it felt like you was falling.

This was not her first time to be tied even. There was the events back in Johnsburg she tried not to ruminate on. Yeah when the evil came down it was as if there was no longer any rules nor basic measures of human decency—that was how it felt.

The Jack voices moved about in the darkness and came closer again and she could make out snatches of it—

feed her up an' maid's worth more than the note but

She strained against the ropes but they would not give at all and she knew that tonight she could die or worse could happen.

Silence again.

She breathed deep and hard. She made the slow droning sound. She was tied at the ankles and wrists in front with her hands on her belly clasped and it came to her now she was arrayed on the wagon like the dead laid out for the paying of last respects—

So what would they make of her once it was all said and done and was it really such a sad story in the finish?

She was not so young any more. She'd had some high times. There had been laughter and plenty of it. She had known love if only for the one time but it was for real. Maybe he would come out of it okay too she'd heard of more than one Lazarus act in her time. The longer the silence held the more she grew easy with the idea of death coming down on this night and she could almost welcome it in fact—

It was gonna be just like stepping through a door. She knew that if he lived he would not forget her and in that way she would hang around still and if he died they'd be together like they were sworn.

On the fall of this last thought came the gunshot and the horses spooked and lurched and the echo of the shot played out as though forever on the cold black air.

Then the horses settled again.

And the silence got put back together.

A single set of bootsteps came back and climbed up the wagon and this murderous Jack was breathing hard up there now and he was panicked for sure and the horses got turned all the way around and they set off again in a new direction.

NINE

Witchcraft in Idaho

As it turned out the broad celestial plain the Swede
Bergman's house looked down upon was located just
a few miles south of Pocatello in the Disputed Territory of Idaho and it was on the shortest day of the year
that the pale sombre boy fetched the palomino back
there from the Perpetual Hotel livery. At Tom Rourke's
approach the horse wore a look of severe moral injury
about the teeth and jaws and she turned her head from
him entirely when he put a hand to her and would not
relent to his touch nor pleadings.

Ah lay it on with a fucken shovel, why don't you? he
said.

Feeling breathless and weak still in the vaporous
air of the season and his circumstance, he stroked the

horse a while and spoke to her with an amount of honest feeling—

He said that he could recognise the low spirit of abandonment when he saw it. He had known such a spirit himself and more than one time. He said the most important thing was they should get out on the trail. All told the Cornish only had a few days' start on them and he could reckon well enough the direction to follow. He could reckon it by feel and intuition, he said, and by methods inexpressible.

The horse seemed to take this in and after a further amount of flattery and a measure of unspoken connivance between them difficult to put in the form of words she became resigned to their course.

Tom Rourke set his pack and climbed up on the note of a deep sighing ache and fuck it if he didn't sound like a man at last to his own ear and with a suave and potent snapping of the rein he turned the palomino's head once more in the direction of Butte, or the Black Heart of Montana, as it was so-called at the time by writing men with a penchant for the high style.

The old man and the sombre boy watched on with a hangdog look matched in perfect facsimile as he rode out. The look suggested that no more hopeless expedition could be mounted by a young man but even so they understood the journey for a necessary one. Love's hard insistences are known even to the deathlorn, and perhaps especially so, with death being no more than the initiation of grief, and grief being no more than the mark of love's inevitable loss.

Tom Rourke waved a grateful farewell to the pair but they did not return the gesture at all. He had offered money for the nursing and the good medicine but they would not take it, not a dollar nor a cent, for they would be to no man beholden.

Which was the way of the Swedes apparently.

His heart was full as he left the district. The pain of his separation from Polly Gillespie was matched by the cold thrill of adventure and he'd admit as much. The fact was he had offered himself at last to the world of fate and it had not killed him off yet and he had hope even yet.

He rode first at a northeasterly tack to avoid the environs of Pocatello, which he would incline to consider a bad-luck town now and forever on. He came down closer to the river then and rode contrary to it and he rode for hours without stopping. The day was fine and clear but short in duration at the low ebbing of the year and it darkened quickly. He rode on regardless as the night was clear and full of stars and the horse had plenty left in her and then some again and they made up ground.

In the scheming of the night the world came down to a new hard clarity. He had never had a task so sharply defined in his life before, never this weight of purpose, not this fury of intent. He kept the horse at a gallant clip. They rode the blue starlit realm of the wintertime. Against them in night silvers the Pontneuf river ran.

Yes and one day you too might ride through such a place thinking you got it bad but the place will let you know quick enough there were others that rode through here before and they had it plenty worse—night in the Territory went past vaguely at the edges like a faint mournful music.

At length the white limbs of the birchwood appeared in the dark to say that the night dissolved. He had reached the forest grounds of the Nez Percé again. The jewels of ice that hung from the stripped branches had a blue glister in the morning light. The place was strung also with old miseries and remorse. He stopped a while to rest and he consulted with the palomino and she was settled and iron now in her resolve.

I'll stay about the same way if I can, Tom Rourke said, and he watched himself from above as he rode on.

———

And rode on into the late morning and then stopped again and built a small fire and sat with it and smoked. He allowed his thoughts to hover as they would, and even dishonourably—

He had not known of Polly Gillespie's existence the October gone. He had not seen her game smile. He had not been made giddy of mind by her crooked laugh. He had not listened to her heartbeat and the way it skittered madly off the tracks sometimes in the dead of night. Why shouldn't he make out west and try to forget her now? He had forgotten much else before.

But quickly he knew it was not possible to be swayed from his course and he was awestruck to know it. He had no longer free will, not in this life. He rose again and stamped out the fire and rode on.

———

He must be free in his movement. He must allow himself to be steered. Resting on the fall of this thought in the thin heat of the winter sun he closed his eyes for a moment and heard of another horse's approach and it came closer and he was at once at ease with the feeling of its approach—

He opened his eyes and saw it was a lone horseman that came riding.

They acknowledged each other carefully at a short distance.

The horseman rode to and quieted his horse and climbed down.

He looked at Tom Rourke for a long while and he was in no rush to offer comment one way or the other. He was a calm old dude maybe in his high fifties with a serene and piercing foxlight to the eyes. He wore a heap of weather and a troutbrown corduroy longcoat. He made a slow diagnosis of the situation, and at last remarked—

You got the look of trouble times, son.

Tom Rourke acknowledged that such was the case and he climbed down also and they smoked for a while.

He told the man who he was and who it was that he was looking for. He felt an odd comfort in talking to the stranger. He took the story right back. He took it back as far as the photographic studio of the lunatic Lonegan Crane. He hadn't been looking for any trouble, he said.

She was the man's wife, legit?

Yeah but of very recent times.

That makes the differ, you reckon?

She didn't know the buck from Adam.

Okay.

There wasn't two days in it.

I hear you.

She was only off the train.

And that gives you the right?

Not a question of right.

Uh-huh.

There was no choice to it.

You ain't the sort has to go lookin for trouble, are you, son?

No sir.

Just kinda finds you, don't it?

I suppose it does.

Yeah, the stranger said. You got that kind of face.

I didn't ask to be born like it, Tom Rourke said.

None of us do, son.

The horseman considered his cupped smoke for a long moment and drew on it and exhaled a thoughtful bluesmoke and gazed through the smoke into the forest sinister—

These men that got sent out?

Jacks.

You sure of that?

I know a Cornish when I see one.

You heard of these men in Butte?

Not in the particular. Of the kind.

Got 'emselves a name for gunplay, don't they?

Some of 'em do.

You get a good look at these men?

I'd pick 'em out. The two that's livin anyhow.

The stranger looked away into the hatchwork of the forest again as though for an explanatory gloss on the story and then he turned and considered Tom Rourke with the same calm deliberation—

I don't believe you're bad-hearted, son.

No sir I am not.

All right then.

The stranger consulted the trees for another unhurried moment and Tom Rourke envied the deliberate style of the oldtimer as he thought it all out at his leisure and he looked back from the trees then and squinted—

How you figure on findin this woman?

If they're headed back for Butte, I think she'll try and slow it. She'd know to try and slow it.

Okay.

Figure I can catch up.

And then?

I just . . .

Yeah?

I just . . . got to let it play out the way it's gonna play out.

You're gonna let it play out, the stranger said, the way it's gonna play out?

That's right.

You'll forgive me a broad remark, son?

I will.

This ain't been worked out for shit.

I'll grant you as much.

How long they got as a start on you?

Best part of a week.

And it's a professional team we're talkin about?

Seems that way.

Actin on a writ note?

So far as I believe.

Then why you reckon she ain't locked up in a back-room of her old husband's house by now gettin fed a hank of dry bread for supper and a pretty little bell to her ankle tied?

I just got a feelin about it.

You just got a feelin?

Yessir.

Guess I heard it all now.

The stranger went to his haunches. He cast a mean glance on the country as though in exasperation at the calamities it routinely presented. He butted out his smoke. Tom Rourke sensed that the man was working up to something, and he was right—

You think things are directed, don't you, son?

How'd you mean?

I mean by hands unguessable.

I suppose I do believe that. Yes I do.

Well I been directed here to tell you that that right there is an insane delusion of the mind.

I hear you.

And it's the kind could land you in a whole shitpile of botheration.

No doubt to it.

And tell you what, son? I truly don't want to add to your delusions.

'Preciate it.

You got plenty already.

You're speakin the truth to me.

The stranger stood up then and slapped Tom Rourke across the face just the once but whipsmart.

Shut the fuck up and listen for once in your life, he said. Fact of the matter is you just run into a body might have something for you.

I had that feelin exactly, friend. Soon's I heard you ride up.

The stranger sighed and took the Lord's name beneath his breath and shook his head at the magic fucking thinking of it and he beckoned in the direction he'd rode from—

There's a town back up there called Driggs. It ain't twenty mile back. I'd call it one of those plain-sister kinda towns. You'd have to be born to it to love it. There ain't but the one bar in it and if your luck's out you'll find the place. I drank there myself last night and tell you what I didn't drink too deep. Kinda establishment you'd want to keep the eyes operatin sideways in your head. It's run by some of your countryfolk or so I gathered.

Okay?

And from what I hear told in that place last night?

There's a Jack that's laid up in the town and he's gun-shot. He's pretty badly off is what I heard. Might be a good time go talk to that man.

It might be.

Yeah but son?

Yessir?

Come in blindside, you heed me?

———

He bid the stranger thanks and muttered a farewell and the stranger mounted again and tipped the brim of his hat and rode out southwesterly and Tom Rourke climbed up in turn and headed off northeasterly and he left it a half-minute or so and then looked back just the once over his shoulder but already the stranger had disappeared into the Idaho light and air.

———

The snow came in thick flurries as he rode on. In the north country the world was made clean once more. It was more hopeful on a shortened horizon. He was climbing again. He knew that he would not grow old now. Fear and sadness and a strange hilarity competed on even terms as he rode. He had settled to a lockjaw state. The gut pain that remained had just the rumour of its old insistence. He crossed twice a forked river by the edge of the forest grounds as directed by the calm-spoke stranger. The river was known as the Snake and on its half-frozen waters the bird tracks were written in silver script and this was beautiful. He felt that God was close by. He spoke to the horse about Polly Gillespie and the city of San Francisco and a fine house that looked over the bay and even as he spoke it he knew it for a dream. He spoke to God again and he said oh please now won't you bear with me? He did not believe in God at all and in fact he had never believed.

———

Evening descended with some haste on Driggs, Idaho as if it was of a mind to cover the place up. He rode the palomino through the edges of town with a wariness to straighten his tired shoulders. He climbed down outside the bar he'd been warned about. The establishment was forlorn and menacing in about equal measure. There wasn't a Christian alive who'd have a brave feeling walking up to its doors. But Tom Rourke was possessed of a mysterious calm by now, perhaps on lease from the old stranger the country had with some guile directed into his path, and he told the horse that it felt like an evening that was marked out for him somehow or more precisely—

By fate and dark magic the evening was marked out.

TEN

Polly Wants a Cracker

Yeah so there was one that called himself Kit or Kitto with the broken teeth like someone stove his face in with a bootheel and hey if ever an asshole deserved it and this Kitto he was feeding her up like a motherfucker with a plan. She was tied to a bed in a shotgun shack or shithole cabin of some variety and gagged most of the time she wasn't eating. Woke up in the night sometimes and felt his burning look come up from the floor where he was laid out all desirous and love-eyed but it was worse again if he was sleeping on account of the way he spoke a weird devil type mumbo in his sleep like a nonstop whining and ranting and there was obscene speculations also and these was of a harrowing nature. Oh this Kitto dude was travelling some strange districts in his night's sleep and all reported back on in the weird oldtime tongue of the Cousin Jacks which didn't improve it any—it was all thee and thou and t'other and such bullshit. She lay there and listened and wondered if this was about the bottom of the earthly pit she'd reached at long last after three decades searching for it. Guess he'd only tried to fuck her but the one time and that hadn't worked out so that was a positive. He called her Mama when he tried that one time at fucking her. Oh Mama oh Mama thy's too skinny Mama. Rubbing his wet soft oyster-like append-age up and down against her thigh. She'd been through worse in her day she could handle it but the Mama the Mama was trying. We got to feed thou up right good now Mama was his next diversion. We got to feed thou up right good sweet maid so we bloody well do. And in the mornings he'd carry her from the bed and lay her on a heap of blankets piled near the firepit and set her down all gentle like a doll he was putting down or like a babe in arms but then he'd take up a length of farmrope kept special for the purpose and hogtie her and that was the chivalry right out the door I'll see ya.

———

She'd lie there and stare into the flames and it was a case of here we go again Lord Jesus I must have done something seriously fucking foul in a past life say what? But she found she could sleep through most of the mornings even hogtied the way a body gets used to most anything in the hardscrabble times. Kit or Kitto he'd disappear from the shack then and come back an hour or two later with more and more provisions every day wherever he was fetchin them back from. She'd be lifted from the floor like the first prize princess and tied to a straight-back chair and the gag loosened and he'd feed her jack-cheese and bread and heated beans and he'd fry up slice potatoes over the fire and those'd go down the hatch and then there'd be sweetcake and milky tea with several spoons of white sugar added. She could be two goddamn hours in the eating and he'd still be comin out with more of the jackcheese like hey there pretty maid thy wants a cracker? This was going on for half a week now. She could feel it on her middle and ass already. Well then the gag was put back on and the system as it got worked out she'd to stomp once on the floor for pissin and twice for the other and she was stompin twice by day and twice by night was the traumatic fact of the situation. He'd take her round back then to an outhouse as designed by some Luciferian entity was her opinion and give her a few pages of the *Idaho World* to work with and it was a thrill of pride that went through her the day she saw her own image looking back at her from one of those pages and Tom Rourke's beside in a photograph she'd never seen before and he was younger in it and looked like a choir boy who'd taken a wrong turn in life. She hid the page away for the company of it. She squatted in there amid the spiders and mystery rustlins and Kitto stood outside all decorous but with the gun to hand. He'd only the one gun that she was counting. It was a Winchester rifle. She was watching all the while and waiting on her chance if it came. Maybe if he had another try at fucking her. Maybe in the heat of passion if she got herself fat enough to harden up the oyster so's he could have another shot at it.

She made out what she could of the country thereabouts. The shack was close to a wood in a bleak lonesome winters field and there was running water nearby and it was low hills eastering. Each time she was walked back from the outhouse she listened for Tom Rourke's approach— she knew that he was alive and she knew that he was coming and she would need to help him somehow.

———

She couldn't but figure it for the Christmastime and that was fucked up as all bejesus to think about. Oh this is surely a season of Noël for the all-time annals, Polly Gillespie, when you're lying hogtied in a shotgun shack somewhere in the Idaho Territory gettin fed up like a vealcalf by a toothlackin Cornish gunsman of extreme mental dubiety and the wind is pickin up outside and offerin its slow yearnsome tales—go sell 'em somewhere else, fucker, I'm stocked—and you're waitin on your sworn lover to come and find you and the fuck where is that boy? Sombre moments yeah for sure but she was never one for wallowing.

***

And the dude Kitto he'd just sit and smoke and stare at her for such a long time but even if she was tied and gagged she could still front him with the eyes. She could show that she was not afraid. Yeah what you do in this type situation is you just keep on frontin and keep on frontin.

***

Then one particular morning she was laid down on the blankets by the fire but just tied off ordinary and not hog-like coz it must have been he was getting lazy. He rode out and fetched back more provisions. He fed her up with biscuits and gravy and brown turkeymeat. He sang her a Christmas song too if you could believe it hark the herald fucking angels sang and she kept a straight face on for it just about. He pinched her waist and laughed and got all kinda sad again and sighed. Kitto was of that troubling and familiar type whose moods ran swift and changed a lot. He lay down by the fire then and stared up at her with the love eyes for a while and fell asleep. And the one called Kitto that was his mistake coz he left the rifle propped by the wall and by stretching out her foot she was able to tip it real quiet so that its barrel sat resting in the fires embers and he slept for an hour or more and she saw the gun's tip melt in on itself and take on a new twisted form and it was beyond the shooting now for sure.

When he woke and seen what she'd done was when the real craziness started up. That was when he broke her hip actually. Yeah everything slowed down and woozed out again and now it was like a torture place she was laid the fuck out in and all the front fell out of her eyes.

ELEVEN

The Rehearsal

The solitary bar of Driggs, Idaho hung no name for itself as if such might qualify as affectation of some kind. He pushed through its doors to a desolate stage under heinous amber light. The bar contained just a longhair Irishman about his own age sitting on the rough plank counter with a mandolin to his knee and a whore lying dead drunk on the sawdust floor beside him. Which is all I fucking need, thought Tom Rourke, but he maintained the performance and crossed the floor and leaned against the planks in casual style as though already he was a wry familiar of the house.

Do you play it? he said.

The Irishman raised up the instrument in one hand and weighed it—

I don't like to really, he said.

Why's that?

The Irishman set the mandolin again and picked a note and let it out to its full sustain and with the face of a minor saint considered the fading of the note—

When I play the mandolin, he said, it make me feel like I only got about the half part of a workin brain in my head.

The long idiot note was enough to rouse the lady of the sawdust. She stretched out languorously and by manner was the presiding cat-regent of the desolation. With the thin bones of her hand and no small elegance she shaded her eyes against the amber light and looked up and reckoned the scene and there was a beguiling gravel to her voice—

There's two of ye in it, she said. Cunts to a man.

The lady was an Irish, also.

Ma'am, Tom Rourke said, and bowed, but already she was stretched out and sleeping again.

The hirsute Irishman swung his legs across the bar in a smooth practised motion and stepped down inside it and laid his thick forearms to the planks.

Part you from?

Berehaven.

Which end?

The west.

Okay then.

Without direction he set up a bottle of Wrassler stout and a shot of Powers Special and with the stylish rake of a hand swept back his luxuriant hair—

You a Christian man?

Yes I am, friend.

God be good to us.

An' between us and all harm.

Where you aimed for, Christian?

Butte.

We'd usually come in the far side of it.

Had things to look after down here.

Oh I'd say so.

Business one kind and another.

And who owns the horse now?

Ah listen, Tom Rourke said. We could be here for the night.

The keep named himself a Joe de Brugha of Ballingarry.

The place'd be news to me, Tom Rourke said.

West of Limerick, de Brugha said. Beside the witch's hill.

He aimed a thumb at the floor—

The sister, he said. Kathleen. She marry an Argentine what strung himself a week later.

He leaned across the counter and darkened his note—

I'm not sayin the two was connected.

He leaned in still closer—

It were just out the back there.

And closer—

Take her for a whore again and I'll open the cunteen little face on you. You hear me an' I talkin to you, Christian man?

Tom Rourke raised his right palm in peace and de Brugha looked him in the eye and held it a moment and nodded curtly in acceptance of the peace and took a stout and a shot himself and they drank in a state of reasonable abide as Kathleen lay sleeping. The amber light came from the ancient and rank oil lamps upon the rough walls mounted—they hissed a little as they burned, and the sound of it brought to mind cats again.

You're sufferin, Christian.

I am, yeah.

You're not right in yourself.

Not for a long while past.

You can see it comin maybe?

I think I can do, yeah.

But sure you been waitin on it your whole life.

I have in some regards, I'd say. Yes.

He understood the place now as an anteroom. Held in bleak amber it was a last dim-lit chamber before the great darkness, before the great vaulted chamber that he was certain awaited. Tom Rourke was twitching hard again but he was trying to cover it. Even still he was trying to cover it.

Would you not ease yourself, Joe de Brugha said. At this stage?

I know. I'm tryin to.

They drank quietly for a while as Kathleen stretched out and sighed in her sleep. She did not look troubled at all. There were no other patrons and no prospect of any arriving it seemed. The streets outside were attended only by a deep quiet and stillness. At watchful length Tom Rourke came to the matter at hand but he came at it sidelong—

I've heard of a Jack round here?

Kathleen at once roused herself from the floor—

The fuck is cuntface sayin?

Concede here that she was a character straight out of the briars and we can move on from it.

Joe de Brugha poured his sister a ball of brandy. She warmed it in the hand and slapped it and at once took a great healthful colour. Cheeks lit up like a ripe orchard. She dragged up a high stool and climbed to it and he poured her another. She sipped at it and looked to her brother with about the half measure of a smile and jerked a thumb at the apparition stood palely beside her.

Well? she said.

De Brugha leaned closer across the bar again—

Who the fuck are you? he said.

Just a sinner, Tom Rourke said. No worse than no other.

How exactly'd you arrive into us, Christian?

There was a man drank here the other night. He told me there was word of a Jack.

Not a soul in here all the fucken week, Joe de Brugha said. You think I'm not countin?

Kathleen in the meantime held up two fingers and a set of thumbs to frame Tom Rourke as though for a picture made, and said—

So what's it drag you to the heathen land?

He closed his eyes for the recital. He told by the verse and chorus the ballad of his haunted days, his life. He took it way the fuck back. He left the usual gaps in it. He told some of what had happened to him at the house outside Berehaven that looked over the harbour. He said he went to that house on the bad nights still when he dreamed. He had crossed an ocean to be away from that place. And he crossed the plains and he came in at night and when he first saw the lamps burning for the city of Butte he knew that he'd be waked and mourned for there. There was nothing more certain than that.

Joe de Brugha thought it through and said yeah okay but Christian? We all know the fuck where we're going to die, don't we?

On the flat of our fucken backs, Kathleen said.

It's a natural gift the Irish people have, Joe said.

I've heard that remarked, Tom Rourke said. Oftentime.

Kathleen climbed from her stool and circled Tom Rourke slowly and leaned her forehead to his back and embraced him and her touch had a soft thrum of the electric to it and her brandy-ripe breath was warm on his neck—

You been labourin, she said, in the gut region.

You think so?

Aren't I watchin you?

She reached inside his wintercoat swiftly and took out the scimitar blade.

The fuck is the elf-boy doin with Marrak's knife? she said.

She held the blade to his throat and drew a slow curve with its crescent tip.

Where's Jago? she said.

Jago ain't with us no more.

How's that, Christian?

Listen, Tom Rourke said. The best thing you can do is put that knife back where you found it but gentle hey?

He had found his style at last. He had found the pitch of authority. He settled into it. He had nothing left to lose. He showed the gut wound and said it was Marrak had left it on him. He conceded that he had been fortunate in the way the encounter played out. Joe de Brugha leaned over the counter and peered at the wound and blew out his lips—

That's a reefin don't look any way fortunate to me, he said.

Kathleen licked the tip of a baby finger and stroked it toyingly along the length of the wound and smiled at Tom Rourke proudly.

Like a weasel take down a boar, she said. And I'm lyin here and I fucken missed it.

The de Brughas silently consulted, and then confided—

The Cornish gunsmen had laid up in the town often. There was one of them that lay dying or close to it now in a house on the edge of town. They named him a Caden Spargo. But before Tom Rourke stepped into the world again, Kathleen said, he was in severe need of instruction.

Coz next time a cunteen come at you with a blade? she said.

And they are goin to come at you, Joe said.

Remember this what I'm goin to show you, she said.

They took it outside. A bottle of brandy went with them. With the heel of her boot Kathleen marked out a rectangle of space in the packed and half-frozen dirt. She took her sweet time about it. She paced out the parameter that was made and thought about it and evened out the angles with another scratch or two of the heel and nodded. She beckoned him on—now come closer. She used a teardrop pocket knife for the instruction's purpose. Tom Rourke wielded the scimitar blade. They paced through the steps of it in an exaggerated and slowed motion. The horse looked on sombrely. From the doorway of his nameless premises Joe de Brugha surveyed the moves and chugged French brandy from the neck of the bottle and at junctures added instruction, as though calling time at a dance. And it was like a dance, Kathleen said. There were steps to it. She showed him how to match feint with feint and how to wait for the circles of opening space and how never to lurch and how to rock back on the heels for momentum's gain and how to trick with the eyes and the hips and with sharpness of mind always and how to mesmerise, always how to mesmerise. The great advantage, she said, lay in the other's fear.

Remember this, she said.

The other cunteen he wants your knife, she said.

His chest want it, his belly want it, his face want it.

He's screamin out for it, she said.

She moved, swayed, danced, folded up, opened out again.

Remember this, she said. Remember what Kathleen she just shown you.

Her green eyes they flashed then and were beautiful—Kathleen, née de Brugha, once of Ballingarry, now properly the Widow Borges.

———

On the Teton Valley the fullness of night had fallen. A dank and forlorn house on the edge of town looked onto the darkness of the valley below. It was a great void that opened out below, and it was in this house that the gunshot Caden Spargo was considering his last indignities.

In a backroom of the house Tom Rourke held the curved blade to Spargo's throat. He could not look the man in the eye because death was so close.

Knife'd be a fucken ease to me, friend.

Is that right?

Go ahead now.

Where's the other?

That don't matter none.

Where is he, Caden?

Took a notion, ain't he? On the lady.

What way have they gone?

The dying man's face sweated in the cold night air, and he rambled somewhat—

He turn the fucken equaliser on me. Left me gunshot and to bleed out an' him a cradle brother from school-house days. We done the three-legs race together I an' the Pengelly.

What way've they gone, Caden?

He wouldn't put the bloody photograph down. He been havin one off the handle left an' right. He been havin one off the handle somethin ferocious.

Caden? I can smell the fucken death on you.

Ah well okay then.

It's a sweetish smell.

Is how they say it always.

Like rosewood or wet ashes is what they say.

I know you can't finish me, friend.

It's in the room with us, Caden.

An easement to me. Is how'd it be.

You think I won't do it?

I know that it ain't in you, friend.

You see the knife I got here?

I see it.

Do you recognise the knife, Caden?

I do.

Come meet it with me now, Caden.

Please, friend?

Tell me how've they gone, Caden.

There was a cabin outside the town of Saint Anthony that they'd used before. If he'd to guess at it right here on his deathbed with nothing to gain from the lying that'd be the place.

He left the Spargo to a slower death. He rode out for Saint Anthony. He reached the town inside the night and the best part of the next day. It wasn't more than a half-dozen bewildered streets. A talkative river passed through and he knew at once that she was near. He saw that a merchant store was open. An old man leant his meagre weight to the doorframe beneath a neat painted sign that read Delign Supply & General. Tom Rourke slowed the horse and dismounted and saluted the man—

Well? he said.

The old man turned back into the store without reply

and he followed and with no breach at all of the silence the man sold him a half-loaf of stale bread and a hank of jackcheese and he displayed with a mime of apology the otherwise empty shelves.

Looks like you had a run on, Tom Rourke said.

Again the old man did not reply and he paid the man and went outside and leaned back against the storefront and ate. The old man came and leaned back against the doorframe beside him. He did not turn his eyes to the old man. He knew that he was in the right place.

I'm lookin for somebody, he said. He's a Jack that could be nearby.

Wordlessly he was directed to follow the river north of town. Not more than a mile out lay a cabin that abutted the woods. At first sight of the place and even from a distance the horse became distressed. He dismounted and walked her away through the woods and they stayed off from the cabin. He spoke to the horse but she tensed and complained and he pleaded with her and at last she settled and he tied her to the limb of a tree and bid her patience for just a while more.

He walked through the wood. He took a high vantage. A line of smoke ascended from the cabin and barely wavered on the breathless air. He watched the place for a long while in the quiet and stillness. He knew that she was alive down there.

He waited on the darkness.

His heart slowed.

The last of the light took an ink and thickened.

Overhead about an acre of starlings swung through on a great massed flight and turned and swooped and ran out swift new shapes and fell back again and turned to a sharpened point and fell back again and it was ten thousand birds moving as an entity like a great thumbprint forming and breaking and reforming in the late evening light and the birds disappeared all at once to their roost and a great swell of silence filled the world and he knew the dark that had fallen just now for the dark eternal.

The door of the cabin opened. Kitto Pengelly stood there for a slow minute with a longblade knife in his hand. Then he stepped out and started to walk up towards the wood. Tom Rourke drew his own knife and turned his mouth to a sneer and walked on down to meet him.

TWELVE

Narrative Magic in Old Butte

Through a long relay of unreliable sources the news of the lovers' fate travelled the high country and finally got back to Butte and there by whispers circuitous it went around the bar stools and the street corners and it got even more fucked up and tangled and there was just no way of telling truth from falsehood any more. Then again this was often the state of things up in the Black Heart city.

———

It was by now the Christmastime there. The brethren had succumbed to a period of sodden reminiscence. This was no astonishment to them. They mourned for lost voices and lost youth. They crossed the ocean again in their trembling dreams. Those with the hand for it wrote torrential letters home. They remembered fucking everything. They remembered the rocks they'd sat on along the sides of the hungry hills. They remembered the dogs of particular streets. The girls with eyes of wren's-egg blue. The summer nights obliterated in the fields. They chased their whiskey with beer. From the mountain they watched the stars explode. They were hot-faced and overwhelmed. Jesus Christ had died for their sins and they spoke His name over the rattling of their wooden beads. They were gaunt with the God-hauntedness. They believed in witches and demons and occult magic also. They believed in just about everything, actually. They descended to the pits and these were a living hell and so a proof in the negative of God's existence. They coughed their fucking lungs up. They had unbelievable throats on them if it's the drink we're talking about. All the slurs cast against them were Bible true. They drowned in their own fluids in the rooming houses. They spoke to God in tones that were oftentime argumentative. They spoke His name in the uptown bars and in the cribs of the Galena Street line and in the dopehouses on Nanny Goat Hill. It was a diabolic world that had led them so tremendously astray—they raised their glasses in unison to it and swayed. They could not spend all their money and their savings accrued. They made songs about the city on the hill. They cried at their own songs deep into the night. They were ecstatic in the small hours on dopeblown travels. They succumbed to the tormentations of gowl. They were endlessly a source of maudlin fascination to themselves. They trotted out their stories in these circling and disputatious versions, and always with sombre refrain.

———

Thuswise, at the brass rail of the Pay Day bar, two Corkmen exiled to the Third Ward leaned into one another and in a religious hush conferred—

Way I heard it?

Go on . . .

It was all arranged in advance.

Now for you.

Rourke had been writin to the girl in Chicago.

The maggot!

Fucken reams of letters was sent out.

No better boy for the letterwritin.

Ah but listen? The cunt would take medals for it. And there was pictures sent out and there was more comin back again. The girleen was gurnin into the camera like a lovebird possess'.

He hadn't the money bring her out himself?

Wouldn't have, would he? Dope fiend.

Lightin bastard for it. Says all accounts. Celestials' number one boy.

But next thing? Long Harrington gets roped in.

Poor aul' Long Ant'ny.

For the payin of the trains he gets roped in! Innocent as the fucken day.

Won't be right in himself after it?

Not for a long while, if ever.

Was herself set fire to the Croats is what they're sayin?

Which I'd believe. On account of Rourke lackin the plums for it.

Ah but this girleen out of Chicago hey? You'd lose your salt if you heard the half of it.

It's said she left a man dead after her back east?

One man dead and one beyond the use of his arms nor legs.

Of course it wasn't in Chicago that happened.

The arms nor legs?

That was in the Johnsburg of Illinois.
Not the way I fucken heard it.

———

At a dope roost on the Chicken Flats a philosophic
Métis or mixblood of the northern districts and home-
wards bound after a Utah expedition lay back on a set-
tlebed and from the long pipe took a draw and took
down the chaudul and gave thanks to it and loosened
his bones a while and held conference with the angels
and when he woke again it was to voices in the scrim of
the background that spoke in awed tones of an outlaw
pair as had ridden out from the city. It didn't take much
to figure that he had met these so-called outlaws early
this season in the forest grounds of the Nez Percé. He
thought of them now as he lay dim-eyed and roostered.
It was in a mood of sadness and fun combined that he
thought of the pair. My-name-Tom and my-name-Polly.
They were giddy and green and always kinda jumpin.
They were in love with each other too much. They were
drawn by natures twined and persuadable to a *terrain
vague* was what the Frenchman of the olden times would
call it. It was to a world between worlds they were drawn.

They were headed into this unknowable place without map to it nor the sense to be afraid even and they were in this regard heroical. Death hovered close by the lovers always. It was around them like a charge on the air. It was like a blue gunpowder waft. It was like electricity. They had an aspect of cool affront to life and so it was deathwards they were drawn—

Or at least that's how the philosophic Métis was figuring things.

Down at the M&M on North Main Street, meantime, a hambone was set to rest half-gnawed on its plate and a stool turned on a slow rusted creaking to announce news to its neighbour—

She been found drawn and quartered.

Not the way I heard it.

They had to rearrange the fucken parts.

She ain't been found at all is the truth of it.

My sweet hole she ain't coz the girl's buried and dead already. Everyone know it. The Jack he broke her bones and cut up what was left of her out o' pure Jack badness.

Thought it were heathen parties was what I heard she were scalped but she's livin yet as baldhead?

There's versions that differ. I accept this.

They've her gone to the nuns in Missoula is what others is sayin.

A raw end in itself.

———

It was midnight at the Black Feather. Greta of Bavaria lay back in her crib and smoked and looked out to the night and to the drunk and panicked men that walked the line and she waved away their enquiries—fuck off—she was not tonight for the working. Never for one minute in her life a sentimental woman she was surprised to find that a stray tear ran her cheek. But then again Tom Rourke had enquired for her hand in marriage on a half-dozen occasions at least. She had taken it first as a joke or strange courtesy. But he had persevered. He talked about a new start. He talked about lighting out. He talked about a place where nobody knew of them or their backgrounds and how would that be. He talked about Alaska as a possibility. He talked about Seattle. He talked about the Bay of San Francisco. She believed that he just liked the names of those places. He said them with heavy eyes and husky relish. He tried on different accents as he lay and smoked and tripped out on fancy dreams. As he lay at the foot of her crib and sucked her toes. He was a strange boy and funny and often suicidal. She did not think he would ever leave the city. Now it was said he was to be carried back to it and arrayed for the burial.

Other reports conflicted.

———

The arclamps of the city burned against the December night. It was nighttime on Dogtown and on Seldom Seen. It was nighttime on Dublin Gulch and Meaderville and Corktown. The new bells at Saint John's rang out cleanly and the bars all hooted and rumbled. The pitheads groaned to expel the midnight shifts. The copper was brought up more so than the silver now. There was a rush on the copper. The purpose of the ashen-faced Hibernian brethren was to electrify the nation. To bring light against the darkness and to banish forever on the plains the lonesomeness of night or so it could be said. And so they worked until death the pits of the Neversweat and the Anselmo and the Badger State and the Whistler and the Mountain Con and the Original and the Lexington and the Orphan Girl and the Wake-Up-Jim. The power of the darkness was all the while working against them.

THIRTEEN

Polly at the River

Three months passed. Same as if her tongue had been ripped out by some devilsent motherfucker she did not speak for the best part of those months. Hell had come alive in the here and now and the next spring would be a long time in comin if she ever saw one at all. It felt like the world would never turn over again it had just stopped plumb dead on its wheel. Early in the morning out back of the Delign store in the town of Saint Anthony she broke up the kindling for the stove and the sky above her was the province of some ice god with an evil streak to him and malice in his ways and in the bone and iron greyworld of the Idaho Territory that winter she chewed on some hard new thoughts about fate and destiny and love and death and all of that horseshit and the way it had all turned out.

———

She had never felt the goddamn cold the same way before. She had veins of ice these blueskin days. She tried to take every new minute and just tack it onto the last one and that was about as good as she could muster. String 'em together like beads and see how you make out. Oh the days now were long hard sentences not to speak of the nights and that's when we're most alone is the truth of it for most people is the nights.

The yard out back of the store was as far as it was reckoned she could safely venture. She should not be seen at all. She broke up the kindling with a sweet little axe that was like an instrument of murder working in her hand. It made good angry *thwacks* that rang out on the air like messages of forewarning. Just keep the fuck back from me was what she was saying. The endless angry winter days and the swinging of the axe made her grit her teeth against the memory of happiness and the warmth of an embrace and sometimes she whimpered a bit still oh yeah.

Wielded was the precise word for murderous items. She wielded the axe. Her words were coming back with no hurry on them but it was something if they were coming back at all. The storeman Tobe Delign was a mute anyhow so it wasn't like they were fixing on conversation. It was like the Harrington marriage all over again.

She gathered up the broken sticks in a basket and made for the back door but her hip twanged like buggery still and she set the basket on the stoop for a moment to rest and looked out to the cold plain that ran to the dune hills north of town and tried to have a poetical type moment all to herself about the lonesomeness of this earth and what-not but it escaped her and she just thought fuck it. She wondered again about such a people as would set up for life in a place like this but then they'd shown a kindness to her hadn't they so there was that to consider. She hadn't known a lot of kindness in her allocated time but she would not grizzle about the fact.

She brought the kindling to the stove in the kitchen and fed it and watched the fire get up and take to itself with good hissing spite and that was one of the tiny agreeable things of the day to keep her going. She huddled in close enough to feel the ice thaw on her eyebrows. Tobe Delign crept out from the dark recesses he kept himself toaded away in and passed through like a spirit of the place. They had worked out a way of language between them made out of nods and inclinations of the shoulders and assertions of the eyes. He was maybe sixty years old and pokey at the knee and elbow angles like he was put together out of sticks and he brought the pot to the stove and set it to heat and raised his eyes in her direction in a particular way meant there was a sup of tay coming. She cut up some bread and cheese and they sat close to the stove and ate and listened to the wind out front and beyond—

Oh and that wind scoured.

Oh and that wind sawed.

Oh and that wind sang—

Sang its evil whining song in endless refrain and bitter verses across the river from bank to bank and back again and if ever a girl was going to feel a touch sorry for herself it was right there and then sitting with the mute Delign over a hank of jackcheese and listening to that bullshit fucking wind.

———

She put away the morning things. She worked on the limp as she moved or as much as she could do without keeling over. Needed a dose of castor oil or some goddamn thing was what she needed. She needed the heat of the motherfucking sun. She looked at the old man and he looked back at her and she tried to keep it a soft look at least to give thanks. She was pretty well hid here was the truth of it. They had the ways of a closemouthed people and they didn't seem to be looking for no conversion type miracles either so give thanks give thanks.

They had a doctor come see her early on and he said nobody could guess what such a shock can do to a person in the body and mind and in the long run but hey maybe we'll find out.

———

She was drawn to knives. Couldn't help it. Knives and axes. Blades generally. She was aware this was not a healthful development. She didn't have enough to occupy herself in terms of keeping house for Tobe Delign was the truth of it. The man just slept and read scripture and ate cheese and worked his store that saw maybe a half-dozen customers in the day if there was a rush on. It was out of kindness again he had made a job of work for her at all.

———

She waited out the endless winter. She thought often of the trains west she had taken so long ago it seemed now and the blue midnight towns she passed through. She regretted the very first minute she ever saw Tom Rourke and she played it out over and again in her mind's eye. Saw it and felt it. The cloud passing over. The heavy weight feeling.

———

She thought also of the days and nights holed up at the honeymoon shack they'd named as Providence and they could talk to each other there without speaking. The way the feeling came through clean as a bell struck when they were just quiet and listening to each other or maybe like some kinda bat music how they say that works. The fire was going and they lay down together. Tom Rourke said when he was young it was a miracle they didn't lock him away with the special afflicted lock him away with all those crazy-eyes and hair-on-end motherfuckers. If you were of the kind that was attuned to the peculiar that was generally the way back home he said. Away with the faeries was the consideration. She leaned in close then with her claw to his chest and whispered some crazy stuff and he laughed and he laughed harder again the stranger the words got. It was like she was speaking in the tongue but it had no connection with any god you might think of. She just let it come from inside. She didn't even think about it. These were words that came from a place that was deep inside. A place that was before our world and time. That was a deepdown place and forest-like. And he laughed and shook a bit and she let the words come with her claw to his chest and she was raking him pretty good. She let him know they both came from this same place. We can be in it still, she said. We can be in it whenever we need to be and we can always talk to each other there. He was on top of her then biting at her neck and breast and they surely understood each other and the whole thing was just the kind of luck that don't even come once in a lifetime for most.

———

But now in the town of Saint Anthony the last winter days went by like weary brokedown soldiers at the end of a long war and the whole episode with the Cornish and the captain and the Croats was forgotten about by the world at large or so it seemed and she could venture a little bit further and work on the hip and work on the limp. The more she moved the more it seemed like the pain eased off.

She walked in the drag-along style to find out how her

mood was in the afternoons. Maybe see if she was coming back to life a little bit. Your feet will let you know pretty quick about your state of mind was her opinion. Henry's Fork was the river that came through town she would never forget the name and if the wind let up in the afternoons she'd wrap up and go outside and try telling it to the river what she'd been through the season past but it was so hard to get the words out.

———

Was the same river ran past the cabin where she'd been kept always tied and sometimes hogtied. On the last night the birds outside they were in a great swarm. When she heard them settle and go down all at once into the wood she knew that Tom Rourke was near.

———

Now it became the springtime at last. An expedition was arranged. Without anything being said she knew it was for her state of mind. On a fine day she was brought on a picnic by a family she thinks were called the Allertons a real mom and pop type with a pair of angel face blondeheaded kids in tow. They went to the sand dunes north of Saint Anthony and it was a place like nowhere else just miles of open crystal light and crested hills of sand and dry as a desert air and it was a white-out kinda feeling and she could walk easier now and she played with the little blonde kids a while and they saw their nutty long shadows in the new springtime sun and they all laughed about that and danced silly for a bit. They set down the picnic then and sat to it and ate and made jokes but she found she could not arrange her face for that bullshit or not for long or not yet. Instead she went and walked on her own for a while.

She walked among the sand dunes. On the crested slopes in the breeze the grains moved and whispered and sang. It was a lonesome sound and it troubled her in the mind. She tried not to think about the last night of her incarceration at the hands of the love-eyed maniac Pengelly but it was all coming back again—

The birds settled and went down into the wood and Kitto opened the door and stood there for a long while with his knife to hand and he was ready for it and he walked out.

And there was the noise and consternation and the screams and taunts of the fightin and the birds were roused again and screamed in the darkness and her own thrashing to be free and then the silence that was the hardest of it—

The great dark oily pool of silence that opened out in the night and lasted forever and all time.

The slow dead beats of that silence when nobody came and knowing this was real and not a dream and it must have been the late morning or even noon on that next day on that clear and evil windless day when Tobe Delign and some others came up from the town and found her there all tied and wretched.

They said not to look as she was carried out but how could she not look at two men all cut up and lying dead there in the snow.

———

She could not see it again in her mind's eye for a long while. She just could not run the film of it. She could not arrange the images but she could reckon their meaning well enough. She knew that he had died for love.

———

The way the bodies were thrun down the townspeople reckoned he had killed the Jack and died in the effort. Looked as if a bad gut wound had opened on the boy they said. They told her this pretty matter-of-fact in style. They sent his body back to Butte then not knowing what else to do with it. They were thinking maybe he had people back in Butte. The horse was found in the wood and repatriated also. She thought about the horse often and with remorse actually. Much later she wrote to Con Sullivan c/o the M&M on North Main because Tom had spoken of the man as his one true friend in the town. Fat Con at the greasy morning counter was the only one he'd trust if it came right down to it. She was not expecting a reply but it came inside a few weeks.

They waked him at the Board of Trade. He was laid out on the bartop there. That was their way always it was not disrespectful. Drinks were placed by his chest some draft beer and whiskey chasers and silver coins were placed to weight his eyelids and everyone drank to his memory and sang his songs or what could be remembered of them but mostly just the old songs in general the ones they always sang. I state again it was respectful Con Sullivan wrote don't you worry about that. Mr. Delahunty had done as ever a tremendous job with the remains he was the best hand in the business there was none to match him. It all went off pretty well and it turned into quite a festivity on account of the wake being matched up with a wedding that had taken place same day Patrick Holohan of Cork had married a Margaret Stapleton on account of letters Tom had written for him and wasn't it a remarkable turn of events that showed love and death they co-exist in our violent and sentimental world. They might even depend one on the other. Pat Holohan was quite tearful as he gave thanks to the remains Con Sullivan wrote and he wasn't the only one on the premises with a wetness at the eye is the truth of it. Margaret as it turned out was hale and honest-looking and could take a drink to say the least of it. A fine array of miners showed up from manys the pit. Some Croats showed their faces despite or maybe even because of what had transpired at the Zagreb Boarding House (as was). The night went on to a quite untenable hour is what Con Sullivan wrote he had this fussy style in his letterwriting. There was drinking and singing and by the finish of it there was dancing and the Board of Trade put up several rounds on the house which is by no means a frequent occurrence. Saddest thing of all Sullivan wrote there was no one in Creation would have enjoyed a night the like of it better than Tom

Rourke himself. All the sap seemed to go out of the letter just then and it ended curtly. His people had been written to the brother that was left. He was buried in Butte forthwith and he lies in eternal rest there now in the granite hills.

———

She vowed that one day she'd go to his grave and leave a token but she never did and she had no reason to anyhow—they were in their own place together as often as they needed to be and they could talk to each other there.

———

It was in the early summer of '92 that she made it to the city on the bay at last. One way of looking at it she just upped and moved her bones from Chicago to San Francisco with a couple of stop-offs along the way. Might as well take in the scenery while you still can.

The first months were hard though. Alone in the evenings in the rooming house beat out hollow from work she'd lie on the bed and run through her day for him.

She'd talk it all out. Everything that happened to her even the smallest thing a peculiar-lookin one-eye dog she'd seen dancin for coins and pullin all kinds of sassy tricks it was a way for her to make sense of her life just by telling him this bullshit stuff. Nights she did not sleep much and the nights went on forever. But still over time she came to love that wakeful room loved it because it was here she figured out she wasn't going to die herself after all or at least not too soon.

Also the room had its own brand new steam radiator and that was the all time joy of her life when the year turned. It spoke in its own tongue all mystery hisses and raspy licks and it throbbed like a fat little sungod just snug there beneath the window and that was terrific when there was a gale coming across the bay. It hissed and licked and she looked out to the grey and rain and the minutes were tacked onto minutes and turned into months and years and she wonders what they make of her now the little old lady with dye blonde hair limps a bit in the damp weather sometimes but all painted up and nice enough lookin still at seventy-one years old is a fucking result any way you want to look at it.

There have been lots of rooms. Where she lives now she has a small efficiency a bedroom and a kitchen sitting room and it is not far from Polk Street and handy for the Alhambra.

There is a good mix in the building she feels. There's some other olds and some middle-agers and a young couple with a crying baby on the first floor and everyone just loves that baby.

A little after six she gets herself ready. Powders and paints coz what you show on the surface can explain away a whole lot of life. Mostly now it's evenings she works at the Alhambra seven to eleven the last couple of shows the little old painted lady in the ticket box is furniture at the Alhambra by now and she'll snap at you sometimes if she's not in the mood for it. Throw any kind of remark her direction she'll hit it right back at you. She helps at the concession too and goes and talks to Dan in Projection. In dribs and drabs and ass over headways she sees most every bit of every picture they take in. If she's in a more forgiving type mood she likes to see the young couples come through all loved up with each other and watching the stories play out. Hey I got the beating of any one of them you want to listen up I could give you the best part of it in a half hour. But why look back is what she thinks. If she looked back she'd be eaten whole and alive by the past.

Though sometimes in the night it comes and if she can't always get his voice on account of he had so many she can always fetch up his face and his way of laughing. But she tries not to fall into the drag of the past like the drag of a river because it is so powerful it can take you down. Anyhow the past it shifts around all the time. The past is not fixed and it is not certain and this much she has learned if nothin else. The past it changes all the while every minute you're still breathing and how in fuck are you supposed to make sense of it all.

———

It is midnight now on Vallejo Street. As a custom she takes a glass of brandy late on. The blossom on the cherry trees is pink and eerie in the streetlight. The spring has come through again. Mostly she manages to stay just where she is right now in this present moment of time and on the street below a young drunk stumbles by and sings a song of broken hearts and the song is always the same old song and something makes him look up and he waves and she laughs and waves back and she hopes that he's happy. He tries to pull off a jaunty manoeuvre with his hat then but forgets the moves of it halfways through and stumbles off into the rest of the century.

The lights on the water. The lights on the water move her. She is most alive always in the deep of the night and that much has never changed. The wind blows and the past shifts again and rearranges. She can go there still when she wants to. She can see their fire burning in the forest dark. But hey it's all such a long time ago now and really she doesn't even think about it that often.

KEVIN BARRY is the author of the novels *Night Boat to Tangier, Beatlebone,* and *City of Bohane,* as well as three story collections, including *That Old Country Music.* His stories and essays have appeared in *The New Yorker, Granta,* and elsewhere. He also works as a playwright and screenwriter, and he lives in County Sligo, Ireland.